Titles by *Langaa RPCIG*

Mystique

A Collection of Lake Myths

Beatrice Fri Bime

Langaa Research & Publishing CIG
Mankon, Bamenda

Publisher:
Langaa RPCIG
Langaa Research & Publishing Common Initiative Group
P.O. Box 902 Mankon
Bamenda
North West Region
Cameroon
Langaagrp@gmail.com
www.langaa-rpcig.net

Distributed outside N. America by African Books Collective
orders@africanbookscollective.com
www.africanbookscollective.com

Distributed in N. America by Michigan State University
Press
msupress@msu.edu
www.msupress.msu.edu

ISBN: 9956-558-21-4

DISCLAIMER

Contents

Dedication

To the people who have made me the person I am:

My Grandmother, Sarah Angob Mbaku,

My Mother, Elizabeth Anje Mbaku,

and

My husband, John Sabbas Bime,

You live on in my heart.

Acknowledgements

SPECIAL THANKS GO TO Mr. Aloysius Yiveyuvi (Pa Bankomo) who first told me the story of Lake Oku and got me started on Lake Myths.

The others would not have been written without the contributions of Sebastian Ngu Mbaku, Mr. J. Sama Ndi, Mr. Edi Mesumbe, Mrs Esther Fombon, Manyi Mbozphor nee Esther Nji, Fon Bambi III of Wum, Mrs. Lucia Kang, Mr. Thompson Apea Kwabi of Ghana and the young Novitiate in Tanzania.

My children, Kerman, Chiawa and Akere Bime.
 I appreciate your indulgence. Thanks for all the joy you give me.

To all my friends (You know yourselves!) thank you for being there.

To the Editors and Publishers thank you, for bringing the work out to the public.

Special THANKS go to Aisatou Ngong for painstakingly editing the stories. And to Azah Ngu, Caroline Kilo Bara and Therese Nchami for reading the first draft and providing valuable feedback.

Lake Oku

In the beginning, when God created the universe, the earth was formless and desolate. The raging ocean that covered everything was engulfed in total darkness, and the spirit of God was moving over the water. Then God commanded, "Let the water below the sky come together in one place, so that the land will appear." And it was done. He named the land "earth", and the water which had come together he named "sea". And God was pleased with what he saw.

Genesis 1:1-3, 9-10

Prologue

It was 2 p.m. I was standing at the edge of the lake, watching the wind play touch-and-run with the surface of the water. I could see swallows dive up and down, even touching the surface of the water with their wings. The Lake was a body of blue water stretching as far as the eye could see, over an area of one square mile. Because of the intense heat of the mid- day sun, I could see vapour rising from all corners as if the Lake was a giant cauldron.

The lake is protected on all its sides by undulating hills. It is surrounded by a twenty meter flat ground and grass that stays green and short all year round. The Lake seems to open its arms like a cheerful mistress, perpetually waiting for the numerous visitors who come from all over, year in, year out to picnic on its grounds. People come to drink of its water and watch the wind gently caressing its surface, embracing it, as if the Lake and wind were having a tempestuous love affair.

I looked down just as my ten-year old son lifted his hand to defiantly throw the bone of the chicken drumstick he had just finished eating into the lake. I caught his hand in the process and he looked at me and asked:

"Mama, can't I throw it in the Lake? I would like to see the water bubble."

Taking the bone from him, I answered, "No, Pappy."

"Why not, Mama?" the poor boy enquired, looking up at me with accusing eyes. It would be a minute before I answered him. As I looked across the lake, my mind went back twenty-two years. The very first time I came to the Lake.

My parents must have taken me home when I was baby to show the new born to my grandparents and do the *Born House* which consists of cooking food and inviting relatives and friends to come and celebrate the birth of a baby into the family. However, as I was a baby, I have no recollection of that visit. The trip I can remember is the one, when I was ten years old.

The first two days were very difficult and trying for all of us. At that time, our home in the village was a two-bedroom mud-brick house, which my father had built next to my grandparents. The house was roofed with corrugated iron sheets which reflected the sunlight. The house stood out like a sore thumb in the midst all the houses thatched with grass. There were no lights so we had to use paraffin lamps which I was unused to. It was a new experience not to be able to switch on the lights. The house had no flush toilet. I had never seen a pit latrine and did not know how to use one. The first time I asked to use the toilet and was shown the hole in the earth, I could not. Then when I really had to go, I climbed over the sticks and my slippers fell into the hole. I came out crying because I lost my favourite slippers. I was inconsolable.

There were no taps, no showers or baths in the house and water had to be fetched from a stream a mile away. Worst of all, my parents had neglected to teach me our native language, so I could not communicate with the other children. The children all looked muddy and dirty. Some ran around half-naked, while others enjoyed the feel of the soil on their bare feet. With all my airs and clean clothes, I looked and felt out of place. My cousins were wearing my old clothes, which I suspect my mother had packed and sent home through one relative or the other, who frequently visited our house in the city.

That was not how I had planned to spend my vacation so all I did for the first two days was cry and asked to be taken back 'home' to the city. Besides, the dust gave me cough and a cold. My grandmother who was very happy to have us at home tried to comfort me with goodies like roasted groundnuts and corn. I was exasperating everyone. None of my younger siblings seemed to feel the way I felt. Nevertheless, what did they know? They were all younger than I was, and found everything exhilarating and exciting.

The third day, in a desperate bid to distract me, my mother took me on a picnic to the lake. The road to the lake was a footpath not wider than one meter through a thick forest and up a hill. We stumbled over rocks as we made our way there. On either side of the footpath were twigs and stumps of burnt grass and pieces of broken bottles from visitors who slipped and fell. Although I was tired by the time we got to the lake, it was worth the trek. It gave me an interesting opportunity to witness one of the most peaceful and beautiful sites I had ever seen.

I did not know where we were going. At first I thought we were going to the farm. However, when we finished ascending and the lake appeared before me as if it was an accident, I could not help taking in a deep breath. The breeze at that height was very cold. The sky-blue waters nestled on top of the hill as if it were out of place. The contrast between the lake and its surroundings (which we had come through) made the view of the lake spell-binding. I wanted to run and swim in the lake but my mother held me back. Lake Oku makes anyone appreciate God and his creation.

After that experience, I then settled down somehow and, using some form of sign language, I managed to talk the other children into spending half of the vacation with me at the lake. Before the vacation was over, between my grandparents and my interaction with the other children, I had learned to speak in our native language.

How different the village appears today. All the houses are roofed. There is electricity and pipe-borne water, and the village is slowly becoming a little town. There are provision shops everywhere and small film halls where people can watch Nigerian movies. Given that the lake attracts many tourists to the village, the locals had no choice but to go with the tide and develop. There are two hotels in the village.

Pappy tugged at my jeans trousers impatiently and said: "Mama!"

"Sorry, Pappy," I said ruffling his hair, "I was just thinking."

"About what?" he asked.

"About the first time I came here, I was about your age, the questions I asked and the story my mother told me."

"Will you tell it to me?"

"Yes, when we get home."

"Does it have anything to do with why I can't throw something into the Lake?"

"Yes, Pappy."

"Whoopee!" he shouted jumping up and down.

Here is the story I told him, exactly as my mother told me many years before.

Chapter One

The Decision of the Lake

There was only one method, by which the true ownership of the larger lake could be settled forever. One Fon would have to lay down his life because of the lake and for his people be it the Fon of Djem or that of Oku. It meant a specific sacrifice and risk of their lives. However, this task was not the only problem of the Fons. The people, their subjects, were another problem. Would they accept to let their Fons risk their lives or would they continue to kill each other in the fight over the ownership of the lake? After so many lives lost on both sides, the Fons of Djem and Oku decided to put down their weapons and let the lake itself decide whom it belonged to.

The day of reckoning was set for a *contrey Sunday*, the traditional day of rest in both tribes. Had it not been a resting day, the inhabitants from all the surrounding villages would still have abandoned other activities in favour of coming to witness the spectacle that was about to take place. The villagers came children, men, women, the old, the healthy and the sick. They stood on opposite sides of the lake, not throwing the normal insults at each other as was often the case, but to wait for the irrefutable decision of the lake. From that day the decision of the Lake would be adhered to. There had been far too many attacks, insults, and bitterness, on both sides. It just had to end some day. Moreover, that "someday" had finally come. The hour of reckoning was at 3 o'clock in the afternoon.

At the appointed hour, the two Fons arrived. The villagers pulled themselves back to make way for their respective Fons and their counsellors to pass and stand at the edge of the lake. They were dressed in their finest traditional robes and headgear. Each Fon held a rope tied to a large goat in his left hand and carried a large white cock in the right hand - that kept crowing and shaking its head in protest.

Then like a death knell, the gong was sounded. The villagers held their breath. One could even hear hearts beating above the stillness of that split second! They all watched in fascination as their respective Fons stepped into the lake, dragging their reluctant offerings along with them. The solemnity of the occasion was almost ruined by a stubborn goat that just would not move and had to be kicked several times on the flanks. The Fons took one kingly step after another towards the centre of the lake, each step, bringing water higher and higher up their bodies until finally they sank and disappeared under the water together with their offerings.

The atmosphere was tense and expectant as the villagers unconsciously began mumbling silent prayers to their gods. Everyone was visibly afraid. Each individual's fears were mirrored in the other's eyes. They nervously clutched and clung to each other, waited, scarcely breathing, as only one of the Fons was expected to emerge alive. Whoever came out alive, the lake would unquestionably belong to him and his people. The verdict was bloodcurdling and frightening! Only one Fon would come back – alive. The villagers on both sides prayed and hoped that their Fon would emerge.

Thirty minutes later, the water in front of the Oku people turned bloody. Immediately, there were screams and wailing on the Oku side as most of them assumed their Fon had been killed. Hearing the Oku people cry, the Djem people started rejoicing and firing guns. Traditional dances broke out, accompanied by the beating of drums as they took to celebrating.

In their disappointment, some Oku people had already started returning to their villages, while others stood rooted to the spot with disillusionment, while tears of shame ran down their faces. Then, as if relieved of their numbness, some elders hushed the crying men and women, while some went to stop the other people from leaving. After all, the final verdict was not yet in and even if their Fon was dead, they had to be sure before they left. They came back, stood in their uncertainty and waited, while the Djem people reduced the tempo of their excitement as they too, realised that the verdict was not clear. The gods had not yet said the last word on the matter.

The waiting was long; feelings were mixed, while expectations were uncertain, but high. Could both Fons have perished in the lake? What was going on down there? Whose blood had coloured the blue waters? Why had they not emerged from the womb of the lake? Had the queen of the lake refused any one tribe from owning the lake? Had they made a wise decision letting their Fons risk their lives that way? As these thoughts ran through the minds of many, all noises slowly died down, and the atmosphere became charged with such tension that a knife could cut through it.

At 5pm, when the sun began to descend over the hills, a most amazing incident occurred. Someone was lifted out of the lake, suspended in the air for a minute as if held by invisible hands, and then splashed back into the lake. The villagers could not identify the person who had been lifted out of the lake. A crown of gold covered the person's head, while sparkling necklaces decorated his bare torso. There were thick beads round his waist sitting on top of a rich embroidered loin-cloth, tied like a sarong.

The shouts from both sides of the lake were ear splitting. The waiting was over. No one could say for sure which Fon had survived because no one had seen the face of the mystical figure whose new outfit had dazzled everyone. Then almost in the same way the Fons had entered the water, a figure surfaced from the lake, lifted a gold staff in the air, and walked towards the Oku people one step after another, each step bringing him closer to his people. The shouts, singing and dancing from the Oku people was at first subdued because their joy, though so great, was no longer being expected. As the tempo of the Oku people's celebration mounted, the Djem people mourned the loss of their Fon and the lake.

***

"Why did the lake choose the Oku people, Mama? Besides, you have not told me why I can't throw anything in the lake," Pappy said.

"Be patient young man. There's a myth about the lake which I will tell you."

Chapter Two

The Woman at Djem

Djem is a tribe of four villages in the Bamenda highlands of Cameroon. It occupies a surface area of about forty square miles and shares boundaries with Kom and Oku. The Djem Fon's palace is about ten miles from the Oku border At the time of this story, the Djem Fon's palace was made up of nine houses with thatched roofs built in a circle, with the Fon's residence occupying the central position. The Fon's residence was built in such a way that the outer parlour looked out towards the recreation ground and the inner entrance to the palace.

The story goes that on one *contrey Sunday*, the Fon was sitting with some of his counsellors in the outer parlour, drinking palm wine and talking, when a Woman suddenly, walked in from nowhere. No one saw where she came from or how she entered the palace, or who she was. She stood tall, with a milky chocolate complexion and long unkempt hair reaching down her waist. As the men became aware of her presence, one by one, they stopped talking.

There was a hush as she slowly looked around. Then she walked fearlessly towards the Fon. She walked straight, carrying an air of dignity around her. A few feet from the Fon, She stopped, seemed to take a deep breath and addressed him in a manner very uncommon amongst women before a Fon. No one talks to a Fon until the Fon first speaks to them. He is usually addressed in the third person and never in the first person, even by those closest to him.

"Sir, I am a tired traveller, I am thirsty. Can you give me something to drink?" She asked.

11

"Sir!" the counsellors gnashed their teeth at the violation or lack of acquaintance with the traditional manner of addressing a Fon. At any rate, they stared on, speechless.

"I am sorry we do not have a drink to offer you," said the Fon, who also seemed to take an unpleasant note of her casual air of talking to the almighty Fon. The Fon had not yet finished digesting this indignity when she proceeded to ask:

"Can you give me something to eat? I have travelled far and I am hungry."

The counsellors could no longer contain their rage.

"What! The Fon give a woman food? Never, never ever in the history of our tribe!" they shouted.

"I cannot. All the women have gone to the farm and there is no one to give you food." the Fon said emphatically.

"I am tired of travelling, and I have many children. Can you give me a place in your village to live?" The Woman entreated.

"I am sorry I do not have enough space for my people, and the growing population," the Fon told the Woman.

"In that case sir, can you give me a hair cut?" She asked again undeterred by the hostility.

"You have to be out of your mind," one of the *Nchindas* (counsellors) said, getting up. "His highness gives a woman a hair cut? Never."

Not even bothering to look at the counsellor, the Woman waited for the Fon to reply.

"No" the Fon answered.

"Thank you sir," said the Woman.

"Thank you, *Mbeh*," one counsellor corrected her.

The Woman turned, looked at the counsellor, smiled smugly indicating she did not care about the correction and simply glided out, without saying anything, her head held high in contempt.

"Good riddance," thought the counsellors, as her departure brought relief. They continued as if nothing had happened.

However, they could not forget about her so easily. The counsellors talked amongst themselves. They wondered who she was and where she came from. Some shook their head marvelling at their Fon's attitude. There was something about her which made forgetting her somewhat difficult. Some wondered whether the Fon's actions were the best that could have been done, given the circumstance. Did they not have a saying that *you do not deny a stranger drinking water because you may be turning a god away?*

Some of the counsellors grumbled amongst themselves, but no one had the courage to tell the Fon and risk his displeasure. The Fon is always right, they consoled themselves.

Meanwhile, at the village square, the Woman met many children playing. Curious about Her complexion and the length of her hair the children gathered around her with the candour natural to the innocent. They asked her many questions without waiting for her to answer.

"Who are you? Where are you from? Where are you going? Why is your hair so long? Don't you bathe?" they asked.

"Sssshhh, children! I cannot answer all your questions. I am a Mother of many children. Can I ask all of you to do something for me?"

"Yes," they answered.

"Good children. When it rains you should all go to the stream and catch as many tadpoles as you can. Take them to the hill behind you," She said, pointing at a range of undulating hills.

"Do you understand?"

The children answered affirmative again.

She said nothing more and left the children in greater consternation than she had left the counsellors at the Fons palace.

The Woman left Djem, as mysteriously as she had come. That night, there was a heavy downpour of rain with hailstone that lasted until the next afternoon. To this day, no one knows whether the children caught the tadpoles and took them to the hills or not. Moreover, if they did, whether it could have changed the fate of the tribe?

Chapter Three

The Woman at Oku

The mysterious Woman had visited Djem on a Wednesday. Towards sunset of the next day, at exactly the same time that the rains stopped falling in Djem, She made an appearance in Oku. The Fon of Oku was sitting in one of the inner chambers of his palace with two of his orderlies, when she walked in as silently and as mysteriously as she had appeared at Djem. She stood tall, looking weary but proud. She looked straight into the Fon's eyes. Was there a silent plea; some form of communication in those eyes? The Fon was not certain but he took a chance and offered the Woman a seat.

"Thank you, sir," the Woman said taking the seat.

"Sir!" the Fon weighed the word in his mind but decided not to make an issue of the error. Besides, the Woman was certainly a stranger and could not be faulted for not knowing tradition. Had she been a woman from that part of the country or village, she would have been fined for her mistake. The fine she would have had to pay would have been heavy. Nonetheless, the door of the palace is always be kept open for any kind of stranger, the Fon thought.

Turning to one of his orderlies, the Fon asked him to go and bring food and drinks for their guest. When the food was brought, the Woman ate with relish, took her drink and then thanked the Fon. She was silent for a few minutes. Then, addressing the Fon She said:

"Sir would you give me a haircut?"

Had the Fon been allowed to reply he would have asked her why it must be him, to do such a menial job? However, the rage of the orderlies was insurmountable.

15

"What impertinence! Do you know to whom you are speaking?" said the first orderly.

"Aren't you satisfied with the courtesy already shown you?" shouted the second orderly.

The Fon stopped their tirade with a wave of his hand. Looking at the Woman, he said: "cutting hair is one of the things denied me, because of my position. But, why not?" he chuckled, "Lady, I think I'll enjoy cutting your hair. How short do you want it?"

"As it pleases you, sir."

"The Fon is as much the master as he is the servant to all who enter the palace," he told himself.

The Fon then turned to his orderlies and asked one of them to bring a pair of scissors and powder, and the other to heat some water for the Woman to bathe with. The orderlies would have refused to do the Fon's bidding for once, but for the rule that said: "The Fon is always right."

Nonetheless, the orderlies were baffled and scared. What had come over their Fon? Why had he agreed to break tradition for the sake of a stranger? What would happen if word of it got out? That was tantamount to sacrilege. The Fon's enemies would use it as a reason to impeach him. They reasoned, if they did not tell anyone, no one would know. They decided to keep it a secret and went about their duties.

After the haircut, the Woman took a bath, changed into a beautiful, floral white dress and came back. She looked different, fairer, with shoulder length dark shinning hair, and eyes as green as a cat's. When she returned, the men's discomfort was evidenced. They had not seen the Woman come in with any luggage. Where had she taken the dress she was wearing? The dress looked nothing like any fabric, style or make anyone had ever seen in the village. Years later, in telling the story, the orderlies would swear that it was a *mamie-watar* who had come to the land.

***

The sun had finally set. The palace was booming with activities as the Fon's wives and children returned from their farms. Mothers hurried to bathe and put the evening meal on the fire, while children went to fetch water from the stream.

As the evening wore on, some counsellors brought in their traditional evening respects to the palace palm-wine, kola nuts, game, groundnuts and other goods as offerings to the Fon from the day's harvest. They were curious about the Woman sitting quietly and relaxed near the Fon, in a living room normally frequented by females only for very brief periods and only during emergencies. None had the courage to ask the Fon who she was. Had they asked, the Fon would not have known what to tell them, for he himself did not know who She was.

At eight o'clock, sensing that the men were not completely relaxed because of Her presence, the Woman stood up and smiling bowed in the direction of the Fon thanking him for his indulgence and said: "Sir, I have many children. You have made me feel at home here. I will appreciate it if you can give me a place to settle with my children."

The Fon stood up, beckoned to two of his older counsellors and the Woman, who followed him to the rear of his palace. There, the two counsellors as witnesses, he pointed out a piece of land on which the stranger could build houses for herself and her children.

"Thank you very much, sir," the Woman said, "I greatly appreciate your kindness."

They bade each other goodbye.

Whilst the woman went to sleep in the palace guesthouse, the Fon returned to his sanctuary while the counsellors joined the rest of the elders in the living room.

Taking advantage of the Fon's brief absence, the elders questioned the orderlies about the Woman, but to no avail. Questions flew left and right. Speculations ran high. But the orderlies could not tell the elders what they themselves did not know. The speculations could have continued, but for the timely return of the Fon and the arrival of the evening meal, as each of the Fon's wives brought in a basket of food.

The Fon, on his part, did not have an easy night. He wondered whether the Woman had cast a spell on him so that he had so completely surrendered himself to her wishes. In the process of bowing to the strange Woman's will, he had omitted some vital functions. His wives were quick to draw silent attention to the fact.

This took the form of whispers! The whispering started the next morning amongst the women. The Fon had refused his scheduled wife for that night and even turned down his favourite wife because there was a beautiful Woman in the palace. Most of the Fon's wives felt jealous and threatened. Some went late to their farms the next day because they wanted to see the Woman in question. However, none succeeded.

The head queen, with two of her mates, went as far as the palace guesthouse to peep in the room, but saw nothing. Other women stayed away from their farms that day in order to have a look at the woman, to no avail. Whether by design, fate or coincidence, the Woman refused to reveal herself to any of the curious women.

That afternoon, at exactly the same time the strange Woman had appeared in the Fon's palace the previous day, the Fon was sitting in the same room with two other orderlies wondering what could have happened to the Woman, when she glided in again. Curtsying before the Fon, the Woman thanked him for his kindness, but regretted that although the land that the Fon had given her to live on was beautiful, it was too small for her and her large family. As if still acting under her spell, the Fon then asked her to choose any place on his unoccupied territory and settle there.

The woman smiled, knelt before the Fon and, putting her palms together, indicated that she needed benediction from the Fon's special cup. The Fon's special cup is inherited. The cup passes from one Fon to the next and no one except the Fon can drink directly from it. The cup is made from the horn of a special bull and is covered with cowries held together by the skin of a Lion. It looks darkened with age and is usually as old as the dynasty itself. However, as a blessing, the Fon can pour palm wine from the cup (which is never empty) into the palms of the beneficiary. That is the closest any one can get to the cup.

After the benediction, the woman in turn left a ring on the floor before the Fon, because traditionally, one does not give something directly to the Fon but for a few chosen ones. The Woman then bade the Fon farewell and left. Some villagers would later swear they saw her take the road to the hills.

Chapter Four

The Lakes

Though Oku was and is bigger and more populated than Djem, the nearest market in those days was in the town of Kumbo; a two-day journey on foot or by donkey, and a day's journey on horseback, through thick forests and bushes. Mabu and Ngwa were two cousins who frequented the Kumbo market weekly. They carried kola nuts and groundnuts from Oku to Kumbo in baskets strapped across donkeys. They sold their wares and bought salt, oil and cloth, which they brought back to Oku and sold at a profit.

On Saturday, the third day after the Woman's appearance in Oku, Mabu and Ngwa were returning from Kumbo market. Taking the short cut, which passed through the hills, they were surprised to see a clear body of water nestling in the middle of the ridges of hills, where before there had been no water. They looked at each other, wondering whether they could be hallucinating, and decided they could not both be affected by the same malady. They stopped, tethered their donkeys and hesitantly sent their hands into the water, scooped some in their palms and drank it. The water was clean, cool and refreshing.

Leaving Ngwa to guide the donkeys to the village, Mabu ran straight to the Fon's palace, where he arrived breathless and demanded audience with the Fon. However, to see the Fon at first was not easy. The palace protocol would not allow him to see the Fon because it was not the day on which the Fon granted audience. However, Mabu insisted until the Fon's Assistant was called. When Mabu explained

21

why he wanted to see the Fon, the Assistant went in and told the Fon who accepted to see Mabu, who then told the Fon about the mysterious Lake.

The Fon, on hearing this, was astonished, then disbelieving, but instinctively knowing that one of his subjects could not dare lie to him unless he was mad. He looked at Mabu for signs of sickness, and, finding none, asked him a few questions which he answered lucidly. The Fon's joy at this news was so great that it was difficult to express it. Water! Water in the highlands meant life, food and many more necessities. The Fon rewarded Mabu with a calabash of palm wine, and some fowls.

He then sent some of his orderlies to go out and call his counsellors so that he could share the good news with them, concert and plan what offerings to take to the lake. While waiting for his counsellors, the Fon went behind his palace to meditate in silence when, to his astonishment, there, also lying in majestic beauty, was a small body of water on the spot where he had shown the Woman to build, two days before. There could only be one explanation for the sudden appearance of the two lakes at the same time in Oku. They were a gift to the people from the woman as a reward for their Fon's kindness.

When the counsellors came, the Fon showed them the small pond, held a brief discussion with them about what to do, and they all agreed to set out for the larger lake in the hills the following day with gifts for their benefactor. The Fon then sent messengers to all the villages to declare the following day a public holiday and asked the villagers to bring offerings to the palace. The messengers, five in number, with feet as fast as a deer's, each went to a village armed with horns that they blew, calling people out of their houses to come and hear a message from the Fon.

The following day, wearing the ring the mysterious Woman had left for him, the Fon, accompanied by his counsellors and the chief priest (who normally performed sacrifices for the village), started for the lake with the gifts which had been brought by the villagers. They reached the lake, late in the afternoon and the chief priest set about arranging the offerings. While the Fon waited with his counsellors for the chief priest to finish, he suddenly saw the Woman in the middle of the lake beckoning him to come. The Fon entered the lake as some of his counsellors tried to stop him, for no one else could see the Woman. Had their Fon lost his mind? Why was he entering the water? Nonetheless, the Fon looking only at the Woman continued into the lake where he received a special blessing.

He was in the lake for thirty minutes. To this day, no one knows what he did in there or what he found at the bottom of the lake, but when he came out, he was not only dry, but a red feather had been pinned onto his cap. Since then, it is rumoured that, by wearing the ring and the red feather, every Oku Fon can go into the lake and talk to the Woman whenever the tribe has a difficult problem.

The offerings completed amidst much praying and thanksgiving to the unknown Woman, the group returned to the village. The next day, there was much feasting and dancing in the town hall where various prayers were continually offered to her. From that year, and for many years afterwards, there was much prosperity in Oku. There were many births and agriculture flourished.

When the Djem Fon saw all this prosperity, he became jealous and claimed that the lake was on part of his land. First, he started by encouraging his people to farm near the lake. Then they gradually began encroaching on Oku land. A quarrel ensued which led to a full-fledged war that lasted many years until both Fons grew tired and had to let the lake decide.

The Oku people revere the Lake. Its water is used for drinking, and it is believed to have magical healing powers, but the water can only be carried by using a calabash or one's palms. If a glass or any other utensil is used to carry water, from the lake, it comes out dry. It is even said that barren women who drink of the water in good faith become fertile. Because it is believed that the woman and her family live in the lake, it forbidden for people to throw things into the lake for fear of hurting her or one of her children.

***

"Wow! Mama, is it true?" Pappy asked

"What do you think?" I answered.

"I don't know… mama. How does the woman take care of *all* her children with the thick forest between the lake and the pond in the Fon's palace? Why can't the trees be cut down? Doesn't anyone ever get lost in the forest?"

"You are very observant Pappy. The forest is very much a part of the lake. I will tell you about it" I answered him.

Chapter Five

The Forest

Between the lake and the pond (behind the Fon's palace), lies a thick forest, five miles long and three miles wide. The forest is made up of trees of various types and sizes. No one knows exactly who planted either the trees or how long the forest has existed, or if it was there before or after the lake. From what most of the old men in the village say, the forest has always been there.

People are allowed to fetch firewood in the forest from dry fallen twigs, but they are not permitted to fell any trees. The leaves and barks of some trees are used for medicinal purposes. A few years ago, the government gave permits to some exporters to exploit the medicinal capabilities of the forest. However, the Fon and people of Oku refused to allow anyone to exploit the forest for industrial purposes, for fear of disturbing the environment, the flora and fauna. But most especially in order not to disturb the Woman of the lake and her family.

It is believed that the Woman and her subjects live in the lake and the pond. However, at certain hours each night, the two meet in the forest and the family lives together then, just as we do in our regular homes. During the day when we in the real world are awake, the underworld of the lake is asleep. Towards nightfall when we in the real world are getting ready to sleep, the inhabitants of the lake are waking up to start their own activities. At night, houses, which are not visible to the naked eye, spring up like mushroom in the forest. It becomes a regular town. People go to work, and do various activities just like we do during the day in our own world. The Woman protects the forest, man or beast that lives or passes through it. In turn, the forest protects the lake by maintaining the ecology. As long as the forest is there to protect the lake, the lake will never go dry and leave the Woman and Her children homeless.

***

"But, Mama, what happens if somebody gets missing in the forest at night?" Pappy asked.

"Then the Woman would protect him and lead him home again," I answered.

"How?" Pappy asked again.

"If someone gets missing in the forest, the Woman and Her family would welcome him, give him food to eat, something to drink and a place to sleep. Then, around 3 o'clock in the morning, they would wake the person up and lead him out of the forest, but warn him not to look behind."

"Wow, Mama! What if the person disobeys?"

"Then he will either die or turn into a tree."

"Has it ever happened?"

"Yes!"

***

At that time of the year, when the days are longer than the nights, three brothers - Shey, Berry and Wanyu - went to farm behind the hills. They worked very hard and forgot to monitor the direction of the sun. Suddenly, they realised that the sun had faded and darkness was rapidly approaching. In those days people never thought of building farmhouses in cases of such emergencies. The three brothers gathered their equipment and tried to hurry home, but night caught them when they were still a long way from the village.

They got lost in the forest and went round in circles until, fatigued, they sat down under a tree to rest and cursed their fate for not having a torch. The brothers dozed for a short while, but were awakened by a family, who took them in, fed them and gave them a place to sleep. The houses in the forest were more beautiful and the people had a different complexion. The inhabitants of the lake are lighter skinned than we are with long silky hair. The brothers slept on, while activities continued in the forest around them.

At three o'clock in the morning, they were awoken and led out of the forest with a warning not to look behind. They were walking in a single file, with Shey leading and Wanyu bringing up the rear. As they were going, Wanyu turned and looked behind. It was pitch black. The forest, where minutes before had been well lit, was then so dark, that Wanyu could not see anything. Ahead of him, there was light. He could not understand what was going on. He was a curious youth of eighteen, and he wanted to see what would happen. So, silently, he climbed up a tall tree and sat there. His brothers did not know what Wanyu had done. When they got out of the forest, they found that Wanyu was not with them. They could not go back to the forest to look for him. They went home and woke their father and told him what they suspected and feared might have happened. They then stayed up for what remained of the night, praying for the best, but fearing the worst.

At the top of the tree, Wanyu did not have long to wait to see what would happen. It was the hour, at which the lake and pond normally met to say good night before separating. That morning, for some reason, the lake and pond could not meet. Exasperated, the Woman suspected the presence of a stranger. The stranger had to be found quickly and destroyed.

She summoned all the dogs in the 'village' to go out and search for the stranger. The dogs went out, sniffed the air, ran the length and breadth of the forest and found nothing. Next, she sent out cats, then birds, but they found nothing. Time was running out. Now angry, she sent out bees. They went out in droves, sweeping through the forest, looking under every tree, leaf and stone. At last, they reached the tree where Wanyu was hiding. They found him and stung him to death. As his body fell to the ground, the twin lakes met over it. That was the last anyone heard of Wanyu.

Lake Ake Bambili

Elkanah had two wives, Hannah and Peninnah. Penininah had children but Hannah had none.... She was deeply distressed, and cried bitterly to the LORD. "Almighty LORD, look at me, your servant! See my trouble and remember me! Don't forget me! If you give me a son, I promise that I will dedicate him to you for his whole life." "Go in peace," Eli said "and may the God of Israel give you what you have asked him for."

1Sammuel 1: 2, 11, 17

Lake Bambili sits on a hill over-looking the village after which it is named. The lake is about ten miles from the Fon's palace. From the village to the lake, the way is mostly climbing.

The lake itself is surrounded by low grass that seems perpetually cut, yet no one has ever seen it being cut. The waters of the lake are blue and sparkling and known for their medicinal value. However, the waters cannot be carried by anyone except for those priests who perform sacrifices to the lake.

Because of a general belief that people live inside the lake, a stone or foreign object is forbidden from being thrown into the lake, for fear that the stone could hit the head of one of the inhabitants of the lake, who would turn his anger on the villagers. One can stand on the slopes and watch the waves gently move inside the lake and wonder why with all the trees around, there is not even a leaf floating on the surface of the lake.

A thirsty traveller, seeing the water looking so clean is tempted to drink it, but put your hands into the lake and they will come out dry.

Although it is common on a good day, to see schools of fish swimming in the lake, not everyone is allowed to harvest fish from Lake Bambili. From generation to generation, only the heads of specific clans who know where their designated fishing spot is are allowed to fish in the Lake. They go there, cast their nets and come back with enough fish to share between their families but never to sell. In this regard, the succession of clan Heads has to be one 'accepted' by the lake. In other words, the lake has to be consulted and must indicate its approval before a deceased clan head is succeeded by one of his children.

In a year when the clan Heads goes to fish and there is little or no fish to catch, it signifies that the lake is not happy with the village. This is also an indication that there will be a lot of poverty, ill health, drought, poor harvest, high death rates, fewer births and no prosperity. The sacrifice to be made that year has to be heavy, serious and solemn.

The responsibility of collecting offerings to be taken to the lake rests with each clan Head who collects the items from members of his clan. After that, the items are taken to the Fon's palace and given to the chief priest whose responsibility it is to make the offering. Other family members can help to carry the sacrificial rams, goats, cocks, and foodstuff up to the lake. They can even stand and watch the chief priest perform the sacrifices. But only the chief priest can do the sacrifice on behalf of the whole village. When clan Heads that are authorised to offer sacrifices to the lake do so, they do it on behalf of their clan only.

In a year that the lake is happy, there will be plenty of fish to harvest, indicating a prosperous year for the village. The harvest will be high and there will be high birth rate, fewer deaths and high economic prosperity for the sons and daughters of Bambili, wherever they may be.

***

Abimnwi buried her eighth and last child. Her hair was shaved with a piece of broken bottle. Through it all, tears ran down her cheeks without any effort. But this time, unlike the last seven times, there was no wailing. Unlike the previous times, there was an eerie calmness and serenity about her that made mourners stop and look. Was this acceptance of the inevitable or an assurance of the plans being made? It had been decided not to leave her alone for any length of time, for fear of what she could do to herself.

Abimnwi, a Bambili princess, was the first of her husband's five wives. However, while her mates had four, five, six and seven children respectively, she had given birth to eight children, of both sexes, none of whom had survived beyond the fourth birthday. The respected position, which was hers by right, was quietly and surely being eroded by her childlessness. She could no longer take her mates pretentious sympathy when she lost yet another child.

Not long after the mourning period, one or the other of her mates would ask a child not to fetch her something as simple as drinking water. They would snigger when she passed. How could she go on like this, knowing that she would soon be passing her childbearing years? She had buried all her children. Returned them to the earth from which they came from. Who was going to bury her? Who was going to cry and make others mourn for her? What was her legacy for having passed this way? What about her responsibility towards her husband? Is it possible that after all this hard work, all the wealth she and her husband had accumulated (before he started marrying other women) would be inherited by the children of the other women? Who will feed her or give her drinking water in her old age?

Abimnwi left the house through the back door as if she was going to the toilet and as she stepped out, she kept on walking. Up and up into the mountains. She placed one foot after another, her steps were slow and certain but her purpose was sure. It was midnight when she arrived at the lake. The sky was lit by moonlight. She stood at the edge of the Lake surveyed its still water, looked up at the bright moon as if offering a silent prayer, took a deep breath, smelled the crisp fresh air and plunged into the Lake. Unseen hands lifted her and put her back on the shore. She plunged into the water again, but she was lifted and sent out. The third time, she plunged in and she sank right to the bottom of the lake. Surprised to be alive, she opened her eyes and found herself on dry land, in a palace so beautiful it defied description, and with a queen so dazzling Abimnwi could hardly gaze at her. She sank to her knees before the queen who asked in a gentle voice:

"My daughter, what ails you?"

"I have no reason to go on," replied Abimnwi, "I have buried all my children. My mates mock me. My husband has become indifferent towards me. I have no wish to continue to living."

"Is that all?" the queen asked.

"Yes, your highness." Abimnwi replied. "It is more than enough for anyone to bear."

"Then you shall go back. You will bear a son for your husband and he will one day own the whole of Bambili. But first you must rest."

Abimnwi slept, then got up and bathed in a golden bathtub. After her bath, Abimnwi came back into the room and found a beautiful white robe made of sequins and gold threads. She was scared to touch it but as there was nothing else for to wear she put it on. A maid escorted her to a dining room, at the centre of which, was a table so long that the end could barely be seen. On the table was laid a variety of sumptuous dishes. Not being a greedy woman Abimnwi took just enough of what she could eat then sat down and ate every morsel with relish.

After lunch Abimnwi was taken on a tour of the vast city at the bottom of the Lake. The houses had an ethereal architecture. The roads were all tarred with flowers separating one house from another. People went about their duties calmly and quietly. There was no day or night as there was light all the time.

Abimnwi watched in fascination as people went about their daily duties with more single-minded purpose than people did in her village and country. She turned to her companion and asked. "Isn't there something I can do?"

"No," replied her companion with a smile, "Visitors do not usually get assigned any work."

"I'm not used to idleness," Abimnwi answered.

"In that case I'll see what you can do." Her companion said.

They walked on and came upon a room full of children. Abimnwi was astounded. She had not noticed the absence of children before this. She turned to her companion and asked:

"Can I go in and look?"

"Yes." Her companion answered. "For as long as you want."

Abimnwi rushed into the nursery with excitement. She moved from cot to cot. She talked to the children, cooed at others, picked up those who cried. She came to a little lame infant, picked him up and placing him on her chest, sang to him. The babies responded to her. Some smiled, others stared, others cooed, and the others cried when she moved on. How long she was in the nursery she could not say. But she could have remained there forever as all her nurturing instincts were aroused and she felt as if she had died and reached paradise.

***

Back in the village, the mourners got up at the first cock crow in order to perform the next step in the mourning rites, which consisted of taking a piece of the child's clothes to soothsayers, in order to find out why the child had died. After that they would shave the heads of all female family members.

A woman was sent in to get a piece of cloth from Abimnwi, when it was discovered that Abimnwi was missing. There was total confusion. Accusations and counter accusations went back and forth.

"I thought she was with you."

"But I thought she was with you."

"When did you last see her?"

"I saw her when she was going to the toilette."

"I did not see her return."

"I went to sleep, so I thought she came back while I was asleep."

Everyone feared what they thought and suspected what the others were thinking; but no one dared to voice it out. When it was ascertained that she was truly missing, order somewhat returned to the compound. Actions, not speculations or accusations, were needed. First, the Fon was informed and then emergency drums were sounded. Anyone who heard the drums and was able-bodied were expected to come and help in whatever emergency it was. Many young men answered the call. When enough people had gathered together, they were informed of the emergency and search parties were organised according to quarters. Whistles were given to the heads of each team and directions for the search specified.

The teams searched from sun-up to sundown without resting. In the evening they returned to the village without a trace of the princess. The next day they resumed the search where they left off. They would not give up until they found the princess or her body. People were perplexed. What could have happened to her? A human being could not just disappear into thin air. Everyone was willing to go an extra mile for Abimnwi, not because she was a princess, but also because she had always been kind to everyone.

Meanwhile Abimnwi was so comfortable just staying in the Lake. She spent most of her time in the nursery. The children appeared to her to be lonely, since she saw no one taking care of them. She would gladly have remained there playing with the children. However, the queen sent for Abimnwi and told her it was time for her to return because people were worried about her. She called the companion who had taken Abimnwi on the tour and asked her to lead Abimnwi back. However, before Abimnwi left, the queen gave her some beads to wear, while her companion rubbed her with cam wood before letting her out. One minute Abimnwi was in the city inside the lake, the next minute, she was standing at the edge of the lake. Was she dreaming or had she really been inside the lake? She would have thought she was dreaming had it not been for the gifts she now held in her hands.

***

On the third day after Abimnwi's disappearance, the teams started early and resumed the search with urgency. Towards midday after having been out for seven hours, one of the search teams sighted Abimnwi walking slowly back to the village from the direction of the lake. Not certain if it was the princess, the team came closer and recognised her, before sounding a whistle which was then answered by another team, which then sounded its own whistle and the process was repeated until all the search teams were aware that the princess had been found. Dead or alive, they did not know but the command was to return to the village. So the teams started their walk back on lighter feet and with lighter hearts.

The princess was now rubbed with cam-wood from head to toe. She was dressed in a skirt of multi-coloured feathers. Beads covered her arms, head, ankles, and waist. Others hung from her neck down to her bosom. She looked not like a woman bereaved, but more like a queen with a kingdom to rule. Some of the younger people were frightened believing that they were seeing the princess' spirit and not herself.

Abimnwi looked at the group with some consternation and asked, "Where are you going to when it is not even the season for fishing?"

"We were looking for you," answered the team leader, "And we have searched for you for three days."

"Three days!" Abimnwi answered. "But I have only been gone for a few hours."

The people looked at one another, then at their team leader. But as he said nothing, the group began singing and led the princess back to her compound where there was so much jubilation that the child's death and the remaining mourning rites were forgotten.

Having thought that he had lost the love of his youth, Abimnwi's husband became so loving and attentive towards her that, less than a year later she gave birth to a baby boy and never conceived again. That son grew up to become a strong and powerful farmer, married many wives and had many children. Using his hard-earned money, he acquired a lot of land. His children and descendants were prosperous and until today they still own more than half of Bambili.

***

Many years later, another woman named Awachwi, who saw the prosperity of the princess' progeny and heard their story, decided to go to the lake in an attempt to accumulate a similar fortune. First, she shaved her hair very low and oiled it with cam-wood, and wearing her best dress, she went to the lake at midnight and plunged into the lake, sinking directly to the bottom. At the bottom, she came face to face with the queen of the lake. Smiling, she knelt before the queen. When the queen asked her what ailed her, she repeated a pathetic story she had concocted.

The queen welcomed her and asked her to eat then rest. When Awachwi was shown the dining room with the long table filled with all sorts of delicacies, she moved from dish to dish and chose the best pieces of the food she did not even know. She filled her plate so high that she had difficulties carrying it. Then she sat down to eat. She ate the first morsel. The second piece she took, she bit into it and broke her tooth. The next piece, she choked on it. Somebody tapped the middle of her back and she stopped choking. However, Awachwi did not say, "Thank you." Even then, she still had the will to stuff the rest of the food in the folds of her dress.

Awachwi was then taken on a tour of the city. She gushed at the splendour of the roads, the buildings, the people and the decorations. Then she was taken to a part of the city that was poor. There were beggars, lepers, and handicapped people. However, Awachwi made no comment or showed any emotions, she did not think or remember to give them some of the food, which was hidden under the folds of her clothes. Awachwi and her companion turned a corner and there was a ferocious dog, which tore at her dress in order to get to the food. Her companion said nothing. There was no conversation between them.

Awachwi was taken to the nursery where she looked at all the babies without touching or playing with any of them. It is said that the heart of a woman, even the heart of the most hard-hearted woman, is easily touched by the cry or suffering of a baby. However, not this woman. The handicapped baby looked at her imploringly. Others simply yelled their lungs out for her attention but she passed as if she did not even see them. Why were they wasting her time showing her things she was not interested in? Awachwi thought to herself. She had come to the lake to accumulate wealth, not to do tourism.

After they left the nursery, Awachwi said she was ready to return. Her companion smiled at her and placing her hands on her shoulders answered, "You may go!"

***

At eight a.m. in the morning, when Awachwi had not yet woken up to go to the farm, her daughter went into the room looking for her and found Awachwi lying on her bed, afflicted with smelling sores and unable to speak. The daughter screamed.

Awachwi had been gone for six hours, but no one had noticed her absence. The Queen of the lake could have killed her. But Awachwi was sent back, as a warning to other people that greed is bad and one cannot take advantage of the gods.

Lake Mwanenguba

Then GOD said, "And now we will make human beings; they will be like us. They will have power over the fish, the birds, and all animals…."

So God created human beings making them to be like Himself. He created them male and female, blessed them and said, "have many children…"

Genesis 1:26-28

The pain started like tiny pricks of needles then increased in tempo to resemble those made by random cuts by a pair of scissors. Sweat gathered on the Pastor's face as he tried to hold back the scream, but it tore out of his throat of its own volition. When the pain started again, with no strength left to fight it, he succumbed to it. Pastor Alfred Etuge's wife ran in, soaked a towel in a bucket of water by the bedside and mopped her husband's face with it.

The man on the bed was just a skeleton of the man she had married and lived with, all these years. It tore her apart to see him suffer so much. Why didn't God take pity on his servant and call him home? How much longer was he going to like this? The strain was already telling on her. She had been forced to quit her job in order to take care of him. They had been to several hospitals yet nothing seemed to help. There were periods when he got better, sometimes for a few weeks. However, not long after, the pains would return worse than before. At the end, what? What was to become of her? She couldn't voice her feelings. They had been married for thirty years, had no children, and very little savings that had since been depleted by medical bills. Now they lived on charity from the church and its congregation.

Most of their money had gone to educate relatives. Now, where were those relatives when they needed them? Very few stopped by to find out about their uncle's health, let alone contribute something towards his medical bills.

The pains receded and the Pastor slept on peacefully. His wife could always tell. Those were the priceless moments when she rested or did some work around the house. They had been in the village now for three weeks. Three long weeks during which they had given up hope and waited with deep apprehension for the worst. The village was far from the main highway and visitors were rare and far between. The road leading to the village from Tombel, which was the nearest town, was not tarred. It was dusty, and bumpy during the dry season; muddy and slippery, during the rainy season. Therefore, visitors were always a welcome diversion because they brought some news and relieved the boredom.

It was late in the afternoon when Edward Koge came to visit Pastor and Mrs. Etuge. He was the pastor's classmate, friend and tribesman. He was a successful businessman, who had not made all his money on the right path, but had gotten very rich. The pastor had been his conscience when he needed to talk. The pastor had brought him back to the fold when he went astray. Yet he had never been as religious as the pastor. He held a cynical view of religion. For two people who had grown up together (both from a similar background, and went to the same mission schools, even went to England at the same time) it was one of those quirks of life that one should take life so seriously and become a religious cleric, while the other takes a nonchalant attitude towards life. Koge enjoyed life to the fullest and looked for money in ungodly corners, but could still share generously with the less fortunate. Koge had been living in Italy when the Pastor took ill. Koge still had business to do out there. But when he heard that the pastor had been taken to the village and taking this as a sign that there was no hope, Koge decided to return to Cameroon and make a trip to the village to see his friend.

Pastor Alfred Etuge was propped between two pillows when Koge walked in. He stopped at the door. Koge had stopped in Kumba, the metropolitan headquarters of the province, and talked to the pastor's doctors. But nothing they had said prepared him for the sight that lay before him. Could this be the same man, whom he had last seen at the airport, only nine short months ago? His hair had fallen off. His jaws were sunken, his arms bony, his pyjamas hanging loosely on him. They stared at one another. Emotions, memories, love, time wasted. Too choked to say anything, Koge ran to his friend and they held each other and cried.

"Eddie, they are trying to kill me," the pastor said sometime later.

"Who is trying to kill you, Alf?"

"The people."

Was the pastor losing his mind as well as his body? What was he talking about?

"Which people Alf?"

"People of the Lake."

"We are both part of the village, Alf. When did you start believing in such nonsense?"

"I've always believed."

"Don't you believe in God Alf?"

"Of course I do."

"Are you afraid of death Alf? Is that it?"

The pastor nodded.

"Alf, if you believe in God, why should you fear death? How many times have I heard you tell other people death is a rebirth? If you really believe that, why are you afraid?"

"I'm scared Eddie"

"What are you afraid of?"

"I am afraid of the people."

"What people are you talking about?"

"The people in the lake."

"Are those the people who are trying to kill you Alf? What nonsense. Why should they want to kill you now? Don't you think they could have killed you before now if they had wanted to? Do you remember the time when…?"

The pastor nodded his head as memories, which were never, too far away came vividly.

***

Alfred Etuge was eight years old. They had told him no one was permitted to throw a stone or anything else in the lake. No one knew what made Alfred do it that day but he was a daredevil of a brat. He held a stone in his hand, which he had picked on the road. When none of the elders were looking and before any of the children could stop him, he lifted his hand and flung the stone into the lake. The stone made a splashing sound in the lake 'clung!' then came back as everyone was now watching with terror on their faces, ricocheted and hit Alfred's uncle on the forehead and a bump immediately appeared there. The stone then bounced off his uncle's head and as Alfred opened his mouth to say sorry to his uncle the stone entered his mouth and slipped straight into his throat and down into his stomach. He began to retch.

Alfred retched for three days during which time the strongest soothsayers were consulted, medicines were concocted, sacrifices made, and penance carried out by the family. The cost was so high that it threatened to divide the family unit. The family quarrelled and cursed, cried, prayed, but in the end, as only Africans can, the whole clan gathered and contributed their quotas either out of love for the boy or his parent or out of fear of possible repercussions on themselves and their family. All the ancestors were appeased, the gods satisfied with many jugs of palm wine as the blood of countless rams flowed.

At last, Alfred vomited the stone, but his uncle had the bump on his forehead, the exact size of the stone, until the day he died. Many would later wonder whether Alfred's uncle also experienced the wrath of the lake because he was the one who had accompanied his nephew to the lake, and should therefore, have taken better care of him.

***

"If the inhabitants of the Lake did not kill you then, why do you think they want to now?" asked Koge.

"They refused me water, Eddie," the pastor whispered.

***

Every Bakossi native with any notion of history or tradition understands the significance of the lake denying somebody water.

The Bakossi people came from an eponymous ancestor called Ngweh. Ngweh according to legend, the greatest hunter who ever lived went hunting on the slopes of the Mwanenguba Mountains. The Mwanenguba Mountains are found in the Kupe-Mwanenguba division, one of the four divisions of the Southwest province of Cameroon. Found in the forest region of Anglophone Cameroon, the area is rich with wild life. The volcanic soil of the region is fertile and needs little effort to cultivate it.

It was not a particularly good day for hunting. Ngweh had been out at 4:00 a.m. and it was getting to 6:00p.m. His bag was not yet full. Tired, hungry and deponent, he sat beneath a Baobab tree to eat and rest. He had hardly closed his eyes or so he thought than he was startled by the presence of what he assumed was a big animal close-by. He opened his eyes to stare into the face of the most beautiful woman he had ever seen. When he tried to touch her, she disappeared.

Ngweh could not go back to sleep. He was seized with such feelings and longings he could not explain. All he knew was that he wanted that woman. He forgot about the game that he had come to hunt. He went out now looking for his soul mate. For three days and three nights, he looked. Sometimes he thought he saw her. Then she disappeared again. He was tired, hungry and thirsty but could not bear the thought of going home without her. On the third day, he found her sleeping underneath the shade of a palm tree. He woke her up gently, and professed his love for her. As he spoke, she too fell in love with him. Her name was Sumejang. Ngweh and Sumejang married and begot twelve children.

During a certain period of Ngweh and Sumejang's lives, *Kounteka,* a scabrous supernatural being, came and told Ngweh that there was going to be a flood, and that if he and his family did not enter a certain kind of box, they would perish. So Ngweh made an ark, into which he and his entire family, and all the animals which he could find, took shelter. The flood came and went. At the end of the flood, Ngweh found himself surrounded by hills. Ngweh and his family, and the living things with them, left the ark, and settled down some distance from the site of the ark. His children married, multiplied, and his descendants grew.

The twin lakes of the Mwanenguba are believed to be the site where the ark rested. Outside the lakes, there is an outlet where the kilt of the ark built by the great hunter, can still be seen to this day.

Lake Mwanenguba is a twin lake nestling in a valley surrounded by a ridge of hills. Of the twin lakes, one is male and one is female. A V- shaped strip of land not measuring up to fifty meters separates both lakes. The

Mwanenguba plains are surrounded by winding mountains. From the air, the lakes resemble a body of water gently nestled in a man-made boulder. The areas around the lakes are green and lush fertile lands where crops can be cultivated all year round. But no one is allowed to farm within a certain radius of the plains.

The villages which surround the plains Nkongsamba, Melon, Mwemba, Ngafor and Bello are in the French speaking part of Cameroon. They all have entrances into the plains where the twin lakes of the Mwanenguba can be found. Yet unlike most African villages, there has never been a quarrel over the ownership of the lake. This peaceful coexistence may result from the fact that all villages around the lakes originate from Ngweh, the eponymous ancestor of the Bakossi people.

Without any conscious efforts on the part of the people, the plains of Lake Mwanenguba are astonishingly, the most beautiful and refreshing scenery in the whole region. It has become a tourist attraction, as people come from as far away as Canada, Europe and America to watch the scenery and breathe its refreshing air.

The female lake is shaped like a bean, and is surrounded by flowers. It has an outlet and is easily accessible to people who are allowed to come and fish or swim in its waters. The waters are not known to have any medicinal values. But as with every lake, the natives believe that the bottom of the lake is inhabited.

The male lake on the other hand, has a circular shape and is buried inside rocks with steep and sharp edges protecting and preventing access to it. It has one entrance and its only outlet is into the female lake. Nothing, not even leaves, man, or animals can access the male lake, whose waters are deep and dark.

At a certain point in their history, it is believed it rained for days, on end, over-flooding the banks of the male lake,

"Bongan," chasing away the frightened villagers. The elders of the village confronted the lake, and asked, "Are you coming to finish our goats and sheep?" In response, the lake receded but instead of going back to its original site, it went off to its present site at the Mwanenguba plains leaving a crater in the original place.

Had the Bakossi people made a covenant, with the deity of their lakes never to be threatened with a flood again? It is believed so. The lakes protect them and they in turn respect and adhere to the rules and laws of the "people" residing inside the lakes.

Said to be the mainstay of the strong inhabitants of the underworld, the male lake is mysterious, and its waters are of medicinal value to the people. The waters of the male lake cannot be carried by anyone, except during special circumstances. There are only two people at any given time who can carry water from the male lake. Two chief priests from specific clans in the entire village can beg for water from the lake.

One of these chief Priests, takes a container at a specific time, on particular days of the week, goes to the entrance of the male lake, puts the container down, and performs a special ritual during which he tells the gods of the lake his reason for begging for water. Then he turns his back to the lake. After a while, he turns and faces the lake. If there is water in the container, he knows the purpose for which the water was asked has been accepted and he carries the water to do what it was meant for and nothing else. However, if the lake does not sanctify the purpose for which the water is asked for, then when the chief priest turns, the container will still be empty. The priest cannot repeat the request, but he can consult the deities to see if further sacrifices will change the lake's mind.

Incidentally, no one alive can remember any occasion (before Pastor Alfred's incident) when the lake refused to share its waters.

Simultaneous sacrifices are made to the Lakes and mountains. Sacrifices too cannot be done by anybody or by all the villages. The two chief priests from the two selected clans do the sacrifices on behalf of all the villages and their inhabitants. The sacrifices must be done together by the two chief priests who are spiritually drawn to meet at a specific place and go together to check what kind of sacrifices the gods are asking for.

About a kilometre from the Lake, there is a square stone, which is as old as the Lake. This stone is visited at certain times of the year by a specific bird. The colour and nature of the faeces this bird leaves on the stone tells the priests what is in store for the tribe and thus foretells the type of sacrifices to be offered.

If the colour of the bird's excreta is bloody or red, it signifies danger, low birth rates, high death rate, low harvest, hunger or little or no progress for the youths of the tribe. To alter this condition, a certain sacrifice is made with rams, goats, and many other offerings to appease the gods. This is done sometimes not to stop the flow of bad things but to reduce their degree or severity. If the excreta of the bird is black, then life for the villagers everywhere will be bright, so that sacrifices may not be done; or rather, performed merely for thanksgiving and protection.

***

Koge held Pastor Alfred's hand as tears ran slowly down their cheeks. The only certainty when a child is born is that one-day it will die. When, where or how becomes the uncertainty in life. Yet the fear man has of death, can only be fully understood by those alive who have gone close to death's jaws and survived. Koge understood Pastor Alfred's fears only too well. Koge had been quite close to death when he had an accident on the Tiko-Douala road. It seemed like such a lifetime ago. Yet, ironically, when everyone thought Koge would give up the ghost, waters from the Lake were smuggled into the Douala reference hospital by his family who used them to sponge him. Koge also drank some of this water, and was eventually restored.

They both understood what it meant that the Lake had refused to give its curative waters to Pastor Alfred. No one had to put it into words. To a certain extent, Koge understood, but at another level, he could not comprehend why a man of God would be that afraid of death. Was death so frightful because no one really knew what happens thereafter? Was it because no one had ever crossed over and returned to tell the tale? What was it that frightened people so much about death?

Koge tried to comfort the pastor. The Lake had been kind to them not once but twice. To take Alfred's mind off his pains, fears and helplessness, Koge said, "Do you remember the holidays of our third year in secondary school?"

Alfred smiled at the memories and whispered "Yes."

Secondary school seemed like a century ago. Alfred Etuge and Edward Koge, the only two boys from their village to have won the council scholarship into SASSE - the only boys secondary school in the country in those days. At seventeen, they were in form three. They had made friends with Mbah a classmate from the Bamenda highlands. Bamenda is mostly grassland, so all the people from that part of Cameroon are called *"graffi."*

During the Easter break of their third year in secondary school, Alfred had invited his *'graffi'* classmate who could not go back to Bamenda, to come to their village with them. They were in the village for two days when they took their friend who did not know how to swim to visit the Lake. Mbah saw people swimming in the Female Lake. It looked easy. He took off his clothes and plunged into the Lake and

48

did not come out again. Strong swimmers dived in and out, nothing. The incident was reported to the elders. Alfred and Eddie were asked to calm down.

If a non-swimmer fell into the Lake, and it was discovered that he did not have bad faith, his body would appear in a 'special house' after a couple of days. However, if the individual had bad faith or had been guided to fall into the Lake in order to be used as a special sacrifice, then he would die.

Natural accidents happened usually at the height of the rainy season when the Lakes were over-flown and their temperatures were at freezing point. But this particular Easter break did not take place at the height of the rainy season, so both Koge and Alfred prayed. Each talked to the deities, telling them this was a friend, a stranger who had nothing against the tribe; could the deities forgive them any transgressions and send out their friend? The elders, on their part, offered some sacrifices. After three days, the friend appeared inside the 'special house' in the village. His two friends rushed to embrace him. All Mbah said later was "Man, you people live in '*Carabot*' (houses built with cheap planks) houses up here, when you have the most beautiful city down there."

That was the last time Alfred ever went near the Lakes. He had a fear and awe for the Lakes which never left him during all his life in the Ministry. He blamed his childlessness on the Lakes. Now, as he lay at death's door, the Lakes were again to blame.

***

The Bakossi people believe that the sun rises from the Male Lake and sets in the Female one. Two days later Koge and the pastor's wife sat on either side of the pastor, holding his hand. The pain came, starting very slowly. There were

49

large drops of sweat on the Pastor's face as he laboured to breathe. He kept his mouth shut, as the pains increased in crescendo and the cry tore out of his throat by its own volition. The pain subsided almost immediately; Pastor Alfred Etuge turned, looked at his wife, and then at his friend, then smiling, murmured "the Lakes" and went to meet his maker at the same time that the sun rose out of the Male Lake.

Lake Victoria

"As Jesus made his way to Jerusalem, he went along the border between Samaria and Galilee. He was going into a village when ten men suffering from a dreaded skin disease met him. They stood up and shouted, 'Jesus! Master! Take pity on us!' Jesus saw them and said to them, 'Go and let the priests examine you.'

On the way they were made clean. When one of them saw that he was healed, he came back, praising God in a loud voice. He threw himself to the ground at Jesus' feet and thanked him. The man was a Samaritan. Jesus said, 'there were ten men who were healed; where are the other nine? Why is this foreigner the only one who came back to give thanks to God?' And Jesus said to him, 'Get up and go; your faith has made you well.'"

Luke 17:11-19

This was one of the readings that Sunday in the church in Arusha, Tanzania. Then the visiting Priest in his homely, proceeded to narrate a shorter version of the following legend. I turned around and looked at Auntie Vicky, a Tanzanian friend, as if to say, "I told you every Lake has a myth". She had told me the great Lake Victoria had no myth she was aware of. Well, after you read the following story then you will understand why I went ahead and researched the story of Lake Victoria.

There had been no rain for three years. The earth was cracked, red with deep gaping holes. There was no grass as whatever grass had been there before, was all dry and stunted. The animals were all shrunken and skeletal. The people fared no better. If the rains did not come, the death rate and cannibalism would increase. The very poor were dying in their numbers, while the few able-bodied young people were moving out to neighbouring countries.

51

The elders had done all they could to appease the gods of the land. The gods of the Lake seemed to ask for nothing, but even the Lake had very little fish to offer the villagers. The elders scratched their heads, held meetings upon meetings to come up with suggestions of what to do, but to no avail.

Nyangono, was a forty-year old fisherman, who lived alone, and but not part of the elite members of the town council. As a matter of fact, he was not a member of anything. Even during the times of plenty, he was poor. He was not even rich enough to be married. He was not important and had nothing to show for his time on earth, which was slowly ebbing away with hunger. He now lived on the hope that he could catch at least one fish a day to eat and survive. His home if that is what it could be called was a shabby looking hut built with mud and thatched with dried grass. It had one a small room which served for everything, a living room, kitchen and dining room. His bed which was made of Bamboo boasted of a mattress put together with banana leaves and dry grass. This served as a chair too for any visitors but luckily for him very few people visited him.

The dream was very vivid:

He was sitting at a table with some notables. The table was laden with food which Nyangono had only heard of but never seen in his lifetime. Only the aroma from the food was making his nostrils twitch. He wanted to reach for the food but everyone seemed to be taking their time. His mouth was watering so bad he could feel the spittle drool down.

He was just about to reach for a plate when he woke up. It was almost daylight. Nyangono could have cried when he realised that it had all been a dream. He had never imagined that the kind of food he had seen in his dream could exist. He was so angry about it all being a dream because he had not had anything to eat for days. He felt weak and looked older than his forty years. He felt like asking his maker to call him home, but even the strength to do that, he did not have. Had Nyangono been born under different circumstances, he would have been a tall elegant looking man. But given his circumstances, and without breeding, he looked liked a bent old man.

On the day that things changed for Nyangono, he had barely dragged himself to the edge of Lake Victoria. Like all other fishermen he had cast his net in the Lake for the whole night praying that in the morning he would find some fish caught in it.

***

Lake Victoria named after the British monarch of that name is found on the hills of Kenya, Tanzania and Uganda. Shared by the three countries, the Lake provides food, for the inhabitants of all three countries. The Lake attracts tourists from all over the world. It can be accessed from all three countries but its principal inhabitants are the Loes most of them fishermen. Due to its breath taking splendour and importance to all three countries, some settlements including missionaries spreading Gods word have developed there.

***

The legend goes that at the time of this story, Nyangono got to the Lake as early as his emaciated body could carry him. He went to where his net awaited him hoping to find a catch but expecting to find nothing, as was usual for the previous mornings, he was surprised when he tried to drag the net and found that there was weight in it. He pulled as much as he could but it was heavy. Revived with the expectation that he had finally caught a big fish which he could sell and buy some provisions, he pulled with all his might and low and behold, instead of a fish caught in his net, he found what looked like a bent and wrinkled animal.

"*Bwana* what is this?" Nyangono exclaimed.

Disappointed, Nyangono was going to cast the net back into the Lake when the animal spoke:

"Please take me home with you."

Nyangono looked closer and realised what he had thought was an animal was an old woman. Take her home where? thought Nyangono. I do not have enough space for myself. Where am I going to keep her? What do I do with her and how do I feed her?

Sometimes a man can make a decision in a split second that will give him a headache for the rest of his life. It appears Nyangono may have been experiencing one such moment. There was something about the woman's piercing eyes, was there a silent plea in them? What was he thinking about? But maybe her company will be better than nothing. All these thoughts flashed through Nyangono's head as he removed the old woman very gently from the net, not because he wanted to, but because he simply did not have the strength, not to be gentle. They started the slow journey back to his hut. When they got home, the old woman removed some fish and potatoes from a bag she had been carrying all along and they had a feast.

The next day, the old lady asked Nyangono to build a cattle pen and he replied, "I am a poor man, I do not have cattle, and what would I do with a cattle pen?"

"Build it" She said.

Nyangono looked at her as if she was out of her mind. Who was she to give him orders? What right did she imagine she had to do so? Was this some sort of punishment? How does one build a cattle pen in the midst of a drought so severe, that trying to dig holes would put blisters on one's hands? Where would the strength come from? As these thoughts went through Nyangono's head, the old woman that he had named *Chumvee* (salt) said, as if reading his thoughts, "The will to do something is half the work done." That scared Nyangono into action. He reluctantly went out about a half mile from his house and started to build a cattle pen.

Nyangono spent all that day under the hot scorching East African sun building the cattle pen. At the end of the day, as he went into the house, he could smell a delicious meal. A well-cooked meal coming from his hut? He quickened his tired footsteps unconsciously. He got in and found that Chumvee had cooked some *ndizie and nyama choma. Nyangono* sat down, ate heartily and smiled at his good fortune. Who questions the gods when they smile at you? He was a little scared but not enough to ask questions. Satisfied, he slept as he had not slept during the last three years of drought.

The next day, when he went outside, the cattle pen was filled with cattle. The cattle looked so healthy that they could fetch very exorbitant prices in the market, in any of the surrounding countries. Nyangono saw them and was very scared but at the same time, elated.

"Where are the cattle from?" He asked Chumvee.

"Consider them a gift from the Gods." She replied.

He danced for joy, and in his excitement, he picked her up and kissed her. He then looked at her very closely and found that like him, she was not as old as she had at first appeared. As the days passed by, Chumvee cleaned up, fattened and without any apparent effort turned into a beautiful slim *chocolat au lait* woman. Nyangono could not help admiring her body. Her company was also very interesting. When he was out admiring his new found wealth, which did not need much looking after, he would hurry home to be with her. Was he falling in love? Who was she and where had she come from to be caught in his net? Could she be the one woman he had been waiting for all his life?

He had not had many female encounters due to his circumstances and did not know what to do. The cows would have been enough to keep him rich for a long time given the circumstances. He would have monopoly for miles around, and could charge whatever prices he wanted. But the next week, Chumvee asked him to build a pig stile, then a pen for sheep, goats and then poultry; and each time when they got up in the morning, the pens were full with the animals for which they had been built. Nyangono was so rich now he could build a big house, buy new clothes and look healthy, while everyone else was struggling to survive.

Wealth in any society brings recognition and new friends: those who genuinely seek one's company because they like that person and opportunists. People now took notice of Nyangono. People, who would never have greeted him in the street before, now stopped to say hi and make conversation. Children, who would have laughed at him before, now stopped by his house to visit because of what Chumvee would offer them. Chumvee herself was an attraction because she was neither black nor white. However, as far as the children were concerned she was a *muzungo* (white person).

Nyangono could afford to marry Chumvee. She was a soft-spoken woman with a beauty and elegance that was out of this world. People speculated about Nyangono and Chumvee and envied Nyangono's sudden good fortune. Three months after Nyangono found Chumvee they were married.

Nyangono was accepted into most of the traditional societies which had previously rejected him. He could speak and others would listen. He drank with his age mates and made many new friends. The same age mates who had laughed at him before as being worthless. Nyangono could afford to pay adherence fees into any and all traditional or cultural associations he wanted to become a member. At the beginning he was very cynical about all the attention he was getting, but as he got used to the wealth and attention, he enjoyed it. Nyangonos biggest accomplishment during that period was making a suggestion to the town council on what to do to please the Gods to make it rain. The recommendation came from Chumvee but no one new. So of course Nyangono took the credit for the idea.

Nyangono had suddenly become a big man but Chumvee lived quietly with him. Their happiness would have been complete but after many months, there was no pregnancy and Nyangono was getting anxious. Then as often happens with African men who have wealth, they have to be married to more than one wife in order to flaunt their wealth. So Nyangono built another house in his compound, found a young beautiful girl and married her. Karibu the second wife was beautiful in a truly African sense. She was bulky, and had a dark chocolate complexion with short crop kinky hair. She was respectful of Chumvee as is the custom of the Loes and most African tribes. Chumvee took Karibu under her wings and showed her how to cook all the meals their husband liked.

New love was sweet, so Nyangono paid a lot of attention to his second wife shamefully neglecting the first. But old and wise woman, Chumvee, knew that an old broom would always know all the corners of the house even if the new broom could sweep cleaner. Chumvee continued to perform her wifely duties. She cooked and cleaned for Nyangono and was available when he needed her. Too soon, however, Nyangono found a need for a third wife.

In a culture were polygamy was permitted and where the wealthy could afford as many wives as they wanted, girls who formally would not notice Nyangono were acknowledging him and flaunting themselves at him. His new friends and some notables wanting to cash in on his wealth were proposing their daughters to him. What could consolidate Nyangonos wealth if not male children to continue in his line? Karibu had borne him two beautiful daughters whom Chumvee welcomed with open hands and heart, but what use were girls to an African father? Nyangono quickly forgot that he had not thought of children or even contemplated marriage before he met Chumvee.

Nyangono added a third house to his compound and married another wife. Karibu took one look at her new mate Ashanti and hated her. The competition was more than she could handle. Ashanti was svelte. She was delicately proportioned and turned men's heads. How and from where was Nyangono selecting the most beautiful women? He really was a man who had every worldly pleasure. People envied him and wondered how he could cope with all he had. As beautiful as the other two wives were, none could be quite as beautiful as Chumvee.

Was it just human nature that people always wanted what they do not have while others always feel that they have what they do not want? Or was it simply the search for pleasure that caused one to continue acquiring more, when everything else was not enough? Whatever it was, Nyangono's third wife brought disharmony into his household and the bickering and headache caused him to start drinking and staying out late. He came home after mid night and would sing and sometimes wake up the neighbours.

Some days Nyangono went hungry because each woman expected the other to cook for her husband. During those times Nyangono would eat at Chumvee's house because she always kept food for him even on those days when he did not come to eat at her house.

***

The rains had now come and there had been prosperity in the village for ten years. The years of drought were but a pale memory. Nyangono was a happy and proud man now. His wealth grew from year to year and he could have married even more wives, if he was so inclined.

It was a sunny day and Nyangono was happy that morning. He chatted with all his wives and played with his children. Then that evening he went to town to drink. On his way home in the pitch dark night just after one o'clock, Nyangono fell in a ditch and hurt his right leg. Unknown to him, during the fall, he also lost his house keys. He limped painfully to his home. When Nyangono got home, the gate was locked and the women as usual were asleep.

The pain in his leg was getting unbearable. Nyangono sent his hands into his pockets for his keys, not finding them, he knocked and knocked and no one came to open the gate for him. His wives were either all fast asleep or they each expected the other to be the one to open the gate for their husband. Whatever the case, Nyangono was left outside for too long and he got impatient and angry. He knocked at the gate even louder. But no one came. Then he limped round each woman's window and knocked the gate at that side of the compound. There was no reaction from any of his wives. Nyangono started insulting them loudly. When he got to Chumvee's window he said, "Even this good for nothing one too, whom I rescued from the Lake, is refusing to open the gate for me."

Chumvee got up and quietly opened the gate for him and said nothing. When she realized that her husband had lost his keys and was limping she took him into her own house. Without uttering a word she bathed and tied the leg and gave him a bed to sleep on.

To everything there is a season, a time, even a purpose. The human mind can take only so much, and after some time it rebels and decides and wants its freedom, its liberty and integrity.

Chumvee got up the next morning and approached Nyangono who had slept peacefully the previous night even with the pain in his leg. Not remembering that he had insulted his wives and particularly hurt the first, it therefore came as a surprise to Nyangono when Chumvee quietly told him, "You have insulted me, you have mistreated me, you have cursed me, now I am returning to where you took me from."

Nyangono did not think to apologise or beg her; after all she was no longer useful to him.

Chumvee packed her things and started for the Lake. The cows broke out of their pen and clucking and mowing followed Chumvee. Then the pigs, stamping the floor and snorting followed. The goat's bleating followed the pigs. The chickens clucked their way after the goats' etc. When all the animals had come out, Karibu the second wife holding her two daughters followed. Close on her heels was Ashanti with her three children. Nyangono was surprised to see all the animals, his wives and belongings following Chumvee. Nyangono's tongue was glued to his mouth. He could not speak, not even to offer the apology, which was now too late. But who knows? Like a man in a trance he got up and holding his walking stick, followed them too.

All of them, Chumvee, the animals, children and women made such a cacophony of noise that the whole town ran out to see what was happening. Nyangono and the whole town followed and watched as everything Nyangono ever thought was important to him, got into the Lake and disappeared. He stood there for a long time, until he himself and his walking stick, turned into a tree, which still stands by the Lake to this day. When a leaf is cut from the tree it bleeds blood.

***

With three countries sharing Lake Victoria, the story of Nyangono is only one amongst many myths concerning the

Lake. A Jesuit Noviciate and a native of Lake Victoria, who was a fellow member in Christian Life Community (C.L.C) in Arusha, Tanzania confirmed the previous myth and told me another one about Lake Victoria. The incidence took place in the summer of 2000 and this young Noviciate was a participant and also an eyewitness to this story.

***

The Roman Catholic Church is perhaps the church with the longest route to becoming a priest. Having many different branches, which have slight variations, they invariably take about nine years before an individual is ordained a priest. The first three years after the GCSE "A" level or its equivalent are spent learning philosophy, which leads to a normal first degree. Then there is one year of Pastoral work, which is spent in a parish during which time the seminarian is being observed. After that observation period follows four years of theology. During the first three years the seminarian is a Noviciate. The next two years after the pastoral work he is called a Lector, after three more years he is initiated as deacon and one year later, if he has not changed his mind and his superiors think that he can become a priest, then he is ordained.

During the summer of 2000, twenty-two Jesuits noviciates were spending their summer at the Catholic mission, at the settlement close to Lake Victoria. They had spent a happy and joyous vacation at the settlement, especially since it was two days before they would return to Arusha for serious studies. They were free to do, as they liked. Half of them wanted to go to town while the other half wanted to go camping at Lake Victoria. The day was sunny and beautiful. The weather was crisp and clear. A day to do anything ones heart desired. The bus dropped those going to the Lake first and headed for the town, which was a little further away. The young men dropped their bags on the grass, sat on the benches and breathed in the cool fresh as they watched a boat carrying tourists slowly float towards them.

James said, "Let's take a boat ride."

"Count me out" Andrew said.

"You spoil sport." James said. "It will be fun just to feel the cool air on our faces."

"This is close enough for me" Andrew replied smiling.

"It might really be interesting." Said some else.

"I think you guys should find out how much it will cost" said someone else "before you go getting all excited about taking a boat ride you cannot afford."

"Who says we cannot afford it?" asked James "we are not yet priest you know."

"Then why don't we wait for the boat to come and see if we can make any arrangements."

"We will need two boats if we are all going to go," said Andrew

"I am sure we can find two boats to hire," said James "Why don't you let me find out?"

When the boat docked, the young men made the arrangements and came to an understanding.

Andrew was still not certain that he wanted to go, but after a lot of persuasion, he decided to go along. Six of the noviciates entered one boat and seven the other. In the final seating, Andrew and James did not sit in the same boat. The ride was fine and the breeze pleasant. They talked amongst themselves and shouted across the boats. The day was peaceful and relaxing. Had God created anything more pleasurable than a boat ride on a warm summer day?

They were exactly half way across the Lake when the weather suddenly changed. The waters of the lake churned and bubbled. In a twinkle of an eye the boats capsized. Pandemonium broke loose at the lakeside as divers went into the lake. Two of those young men in the boat who could swim came out. There were only three divers available.

The divers kept on diving in and out as bottom of the Lake was dark, and they could not see well.

However, the divers managed to bring out five people. Emergency help was called in and the boys who had swallowed water were turned on their sides and given mouth to mouth resuscitation. There were still three left and James and Andrew amongst them. One diver dove into the Lake and spotted a red shirt, came out to take in some air, while pointing the area to another Diver. The new diver went into the water in the area, his partner had pointed, spent some time, and came out without seeing anything. The first diver went in again for a final look and this time he saw a white shirt.

He surfaced, made a sign to his partner and together they both went in to the area where the first diver believed he had spotted a shirt. This time, they came up with one of the boys. The first aid team was doing its work but the Divers were getting cold and tired. Everyone around the lake was watching and offering silent prayers. Time was running out. If the others were not found soon, it would be dark and the boys may still not be alive.

The Divers went in again, came up with another student, still no James and Andrew. The prayers became frantic and fervent. Lord let nothing happen to your servants. Just as people were despairing, two more Divers came in from town and went into service. Thirty minutes later, they pulled out James and Andrew lifeless from the lake. What was so abnormal and stunning to their companions who had recovered enough to watch what was taking place, was that the boy's shirts were different. Andrew was wearing James' shirt and James was wearing a green shirt, which he was not wearing when went for the boat ride.

"What could have happened? How did the boys' shirts become exchanged?" I asked.

***

"The story is that Chumvee and her sister rule the Lake. Both like each other but at times they quarrel. On the day Nyangono discovered Chumvee, the quarrelling had been so bad, that the sisters had agreed that Chumvee could take whatever she wanted and make a new life outside the lake. However when Chumvee returned her sister welcomed her back and there was peace for a long time. The lake was calm, there were lots of fishes in the lake, and there was prosperity everywhere. However, occasionally the sisters still quarrel, and when this happens, there is upheaval right to the surface of the lake. Any innocent person can get caught in between. James and Andrew probably got caught right in the middle of a violent fight between the sisters.

"How do you explain the shirts?"

"I do not know and there was no time to speculate or ask any villager about that. They could have fought over the boys too and when they decided to send up the bodies, they just mistakenly dressed them with the wrong shirts.

"You mentioned a diver who came out and said something about a game of hide and seek."

"Yes. One of the divers said that when he dived into the Lake, he would see a shirt and thought he had spotted one of the boys, but when he came up for air and went back in, there would be no one there."

"Could just any Diver succeed in the Lake?"

"It depends on the circumstances. Most of the Divers employed by the city do come from around there and have special sacrifices they make annually to the lake."

"Do many accidents occur in the Lake?"

"There are no statistics that I know of, but it is frightful because the safety of the people and their well being depends on the caprices of the queens of the Lake."

Lake Wum

"...Now I am sending you to the King of Egypt so that you can lead my people out of his country.... I will be with you, and when you bring the people out of Egypt, you will worship me on this mountain. ..."

Exodus 3:10-12

She was only eleven years old when she went to the Lake. Ngum was spending her summer vacation with her grandmother. She and five of her friends were standing at the edge of the lake when Ngum heard the drums beating. The music was sweet and enthralling. Thump thumpthum. Thump thumpthum. Thump thumpthum. Thump thumpthum. Ngum turned to her companions and asked "Do you hear the drums beating?" The other children turned and looked at each other said "there are no drums beating. There isn't any sound around here" Confused Ngum looked at them again and said "But I can hear the drums beating very clearly and the music is just beautiful" "You may be hearing it in your head" one of the children said. "I think we should go back home" another one said. They thronged back to their houses but Ngum was certain she had heard drums beating at the Lake so when she got home she told her grandmother. "You certainly did hear the drums although the other children couldn't" her grandmother answered. "Why is that so grandma?" Ngum asked. "Because you are a Princess and your ancestors live in the Lake. They were welcoming you to the Lake, but had you gone in to swim, they might have taken you" "How grandma?" Ngum asked "and how come my ancestors are living in the Lake?" "It's a long story" her grandmother answered. "Grandma, please I will like to hear it. I felt like a fool out there when none of the other children could hear the drums beating" "It the story of your ancestors so I will tell you" With a nostalgic smile on her wrinkled face, her grandmother started the narration.

The drums beat.

Thump, thump, thump,
Thump, thump, thump
Thump, thump, thump

The time was five a.m. Dawn was about to break. The weather was cold and while some villagers wrapped their coverings tighter around them for greater warmth, others were just getting out of bed.

Translated, the drum beat announced the following message,

The Fon is missing.
We are looking for the Fon
The Fon has to be found.

The message was heart breaking, and all rushed out of bed. It meant that all plans to go farming were to be discarded. The official mourning for the 'missing' Fon had started. The women would habitually come out of their dwellings with only loin cloths tied round their waist whilst the Princesses and Queens would emerge stark naked. The town criers had confirmed what had simply been a whispered rumour. The Fon had travelled the long journey to join his ancestors. When the whispers started, clever villagers went to their farms and hoarded all they could. Because from that morning until a new Fon would be installed, no one would be allowed to work. The town crier's message was a declaration of an official mourning. Children who were out of the village would have to return and join their kinsmen to mourn or stay behind and be cursed. The male members of the Fon's immediate family who did not want to be crowned will escape from the village (and risk the possibility of receiving a bad curse); whilst those who coveted the throne, would hover around hoping and praying that they would be caught and put on the throne.

It was everyone's concern about who was uplifted to the throne because the ruler could either move the village towards prosperity or ruin. Yet only a handful of notables would actually be involved in the choice and installation of the Successor. During the waiting period, women's opinion and advice would be sought and listened to because although women could not have any direct influence in the choice of their King, they had an uncanny nose for who would make a good king. In most African tribes, the first male child that the Fon had when he was crowned would be groomed from infancy to be the one who takes over. However, in rare cases, if the heir apparent was found wanting in character, either his father would disinherit him or the Elders would do so and look amongst the 'missing' Fon's progeny for a more suitable candidate.

When the drum beat announcing the disappearance of the old Fon was heard, most villagers took it for granted that after the mourning period of twenty-one days were over, the enthronement would be easy and swift since; they all seemed to know who the successor would be. Little did they know that with the coming of the white people and the discovery of minerals in the land, greed would lead many Princes to dishonestly vie for the throne.

According to tradition anyone who sits on the throne immediately becomes the Fon. That is the reason why in the absence of a Fon, permanent security is mounted to protect the throne from opportunists, adventurers and frauds. In this particular case, something unusual happened, one week after the official announcement: the 'permanent' guard left the throne unattended, in a rush to relieve himself. In his absence, one of the pretenders seized the opportunity, and sat on the empty throne. The result was obvious as well as instantaneous: The Elders and King Makers divided into three separate camps in support of their respective candidates.

The eminent successor, prince Nnynyum had been away from the village when his father vanished. He lost the throne to one of his brothers even before his return. When Prince Nnynyum arrived at the village to claim what was rightfully his, there was fighting between his supporters and the group supporting his brother.

In the end, Prince Nnynyum and his brother had to leave the village on self-exile rather than continue the bloodshed. They each left with their supporters and headed in different directions. One took the left while the other went right. Neither brother had the vaguest idea where they were heading to, but they had to put some distance between themselves and their homeland.

The right heir apparent, Prince Nnynyum took his supporters – who made up a faction of the village and headed south. They walked out of the village in pairs. Men led the lines with machetes and cutlasses, which they used to clear a path through bushes and briar. Women and children followed the men. Another group of armed men kept watch at the rear. At night they slept under trees and bushes. They made fire with dried sticks and grass by striking two pieces of metals together.

The second night following their departure from the village, the heir apparent prince Nnynyum had a dream in which he received instructions from his father: "Continue to go South, I am with you, my son. You will find me when you get to where you are going and the sign will be water. There you should settle and know that I will always be with you."

Prince Nnynyum and his supporters travelled through Kano State in Nigeria. Then came to the Bauchi state where they rested for a while. From there they went through Markudi where they came to a fertile land, at the banks of river *Katsna Ala*, and stayed there for over five years. Nevertheless, they were still restless because, although they were close to water, it did not seem like the right place. During the dry season of their fifth year, they built a bridge and crossed over to Cameroon. A few people refused to continue and were left behind to settle where they were. Those who continued with their Fon either fought or lived peacefully with the people of any village they came to, depending of course on the attitude of the settlers. They however made a conscious effort to avoid villages along their path, as they searched and prayed that their god would lead them to the water source.

Prince Nnynyum and his people next settled in present day Fruawah (a remote border town near Nigeria, which is, still an enclave until today) and lived there in relative peace for over eight years. Then problems developed: The Fon of the indigenous people died and the strangers dared to impose their own Fon on the people. The natives resisted stoutly and succeeded in chasing off the strangers. The night that Prince Nnynyum and his followers were defeated, Prince Nnynyum had another dream where his father told him, "Don't be disheartened. I am still leading you. You have not reached your new home. Keep going and I will be your guide."

It took Fon Nnynyum and his people over fifteen years to get to their present site. At first the site looked attractive because the hills provided protection and security. They settled there, full of doubts because the sign to their land of milk and honey was supposed to be water. Nevertheless, they were already tired of trekking and given up on the likelihood of ever finding the land, their ancestor was supposed to lead them to.

Two weeks after the people had settled at this new site, they woke up one morning to find a large body of water, on land that had once contained a small pool. The people had finally arrived at their destination. Fon Nnynyum, took the soil he had collected from his father's grave and buried it near the lake and offered sacrifices to their god. They could settle there. After all, they had the blessings of their ancestors who had followed them from the *Munchi* land to the Promised Land.

The people of the present day Wum migrated over three hundred years ago with Fon Nnynyum from the northern part of the Sahara through Nigeria. Wum is over a hundred and fifty kilometres from Mankon, the North West provincial headquarters. Boasting of over fifteen thousand inhabitants, the landscape is made up of hills, rivers and mountains. Today Wum is made up of fourteen villages with each village having a sub chief who is a direct descendant of the original people who migrated with Prince Nnynyum, the first paramount Fon of Wum.

Lake Wum is a small Crater Lake, surrounded by a ridge of hills, which stand like guards around the Lake. The water is cool, dark and deep. People feel free to swim in the lake. There is no fear of anything bad happening to anyone from the area, as the lake is there to protect its people.

The paramount Fon of Wum at the beginning, made yearly sacrifices to the lake in which it is believed that their ancestors live. The villagers multiplied over their three hundred years existence in Wum, and expanded to the other areas Wum occupies. However, they still pay tribute to the Lake. The paramount Fon of Wum now delegates the sub chief of Waindo who is closest to the lake, to do the sacrifices on behalf of the whole tribe and then informs the paramount Fon and the other chiefs of the outcome of the sacrifices.

Mystique: A Collection of Lake Myths

Lake Wum is linked to Mount Fako which is Mount Cameroon, and the third highest mountain in Africa, found in the South West province of the country. When Mount Cameroon quakes or erupts, the people of Wum know it, because they can read the signs in Lake Wum. Even when it is just a small tremble or cough, Lake Wum also reacts. It is difficult to explain the scientific link especially given that Lake Wum and mount Cameroon are separated by a distance of over two hundred and fifty miles. But the inhabitants of Wum claim that they can usually tell the movements of the mountain by simply observing the waves of Lake Wum.

A variety of fish exist in the lake. Fishermen fish there all the time and there is usually enough fish for everyone to eat, but not to sell. During fishing season, the lake dries up so that children can fish. While fishing the children say, "The Lake has gone on a journey so let's fish as much as we like." However, many Waindo children know that they are not allowed to sell the fish they catch from the Lake. Anyone who disobeys this tradition and sells the fish risks sickness or death, and annoying the Lake that way can cause the next fishing season not to be fruitful. Normally the fish never reduces. However, when the gods of the lake are angry, then fish and crabs begin to leave the lake. At such moments the paramount Fon has to go urgently and do a sacrifice himself. The paramount Fon, accompanied by the fourteen sub chiefs, carries sacrifices of goats, sheep and fowls. The paramount Fon would take the sacrificial cock, get into the lake, throw the cock up and watch the way it falls into the lake. If it falls straight down and disappears into the lake, then the sacrifice is accepted. However, if the cock falls on its side or does not disappear, then, the sacrifice has been rejected and that indicates that another series of sacrifices would have to be done.

The strong belief that there are people in the lake is reinforced by the fact that at certain times of the night, if

71

one walks by the lake and its environs, one could hear voices but not see anyone. Indeed, it is said that if one gazes into the waters at the right time one can actually see people and houses.

The actions of the Lake predict to the people the impending death of a notable, or the approach of something ominous. The Lake uses signs such as the *"Kwifon."* The Kwifon is the highest traditional authority. In most Fondoms of the North West Province of Cameroon, the Kwifon is the only traditional body that can sanction the Fon. The Kwifon is made up male descendants of the royal line. It performs the rule of a military disciplinarian in the society. It is the peacekeeping arm of the society and settles land and other disputes in the land. It is also the protector of the Fon, the land, its people and its traditions. The Kwifon performs sacrifices on behalf of the village. The Fon's technical advisers and councillors come from amongst this elite group of the society. It has the arduous task of announcing the passing away of a Fon and the task of installing another one. It is the only organ with the supreme authority to dethrone a Fon who has gone against the traditions of the tribe. The Kwifon therefore provides the checks and balances needed for the society to function well. They overseer the other Juju organs of the tribe like the Menang and Lum who come after the Kwifon. Very few people ever belong to any of them. The *Kwifon* never comes out during the day and no woman can see it. Even men who are none members are not allowed to see it. The *kwifon* comes out rarely and only does so in very extreme circumstances, that is why it is little known and feared. Meanwhile the *Menang*, which is slightly, lower than the *Kwifon* is, still is and has always been men's deity. After the *Menang* comes the *Lum*. All these secret societies are feared so much so that it is believed that seeing even their light by none members can result in maledictions. The costs of the cleansing rites for any non member who accidentally sees the deities are so high that to be unfortunate enough to see one of these deities might result in death for someone who cannot afford the high cost of cleansing.

When the *Menang* of the lake starts to sing and cry people hold their breaths in frightful expectation as the people know that something bad is about to happen. If the *Menang,* is joined by the *Lum* and the *kwifon* it signifies that the notable is a very high one and might even be the Fon himself. Sometimes the disaster can be prevented if it is an owl, which cries, and a deity is swiftly consulted and sacrifices offered to the lake.

Thumb, Thumb, Thumb, Thumb.
Thumb, Thumb, Thumb, Thumb.
Thumb, Thumb, Thumb, Thumb.

The Fon is missing
We are looking The a Fon
The Fon must be found.

Thumb, Thumb, Thumb, Thumb.

***

Lake Wum is not far from the government high school. A couple of years ago, a pupil from the school fell into the Lake and did not come out again. The parents of the student who were teachers at the school and very religious people refused to perform any traditional rites to the Lake so that the body of their son could be released.

They waited for two weeks and when the body of the child was not recovered, the family finally gave in and accepted that the Ewifey or Fon of Waindo who is believed to be the owner of the lake should perform the rites.

73

Five jugs of palm wine were bought, four goats, two white cocks and other sacrificial items were taken to the *Ewifey*. The Fon proceeded to the Lake, stood at the side and called the names of all his dead ancestors, explaining to them that the people [whose son had fallen into the Lake] were strangers. They would like to recover the body so that they could take it to their village for burial. It is believed that as the Fon called the name of each of his ancestors, the ancestor surfaced but could not be seen by the naked eye. Yet, the water bubbled, each time the name of an ancestor was called. The Fon spoke to his ancestors then gave them the offerings. As everyone watched, the body of the boy floated to the surface. When the body was carried, it was found that the corpse was still warm.

It is believed that the boy 'suffered' as a result of his father's blunder. It is said that while the boy's father was drinking in a bar with some friends they had started talking about the people living inside the Lake and he laughed at the story and had said to the hearing of some notables that all the talk about the presence of "people" living inside the Lake, was nonsense. Thus it was suspected that these same "people" decided to show him otherwise.

The case of the warm corpse still remains a mystery. Many suspect that the boy may have been alive for the two weeks that he spent inside the lake. He may have been killed just before he was sent to our world.

In the end, the parents took the corpse to their home, buried the child, and asked for a transfer from Wum. Since then, they have never visited the land.

Lake Awing

Then one of the angels said, "Run for your lives! Don't look back and don't stop in the valley. Run to the hills, so that you won't be killed."
But Lot's wife looked back and was turned into a pillar of salt.

Genesis 19:17, 26

The idea of an excursion seemed like a good idea as a last gathering of the Class Seven pupils of the Government School in Santa. The Teacher was, however, new to the area. He was not from the province, but knew that there was a beautiful Lake a few kilometres from the town. So, why not spend the day after the final exams had been written, doing some nature study?

"Does anyone know the way to Lake Awing?" the Teacher asked the students.

Many hands shot up. But no one told the teacher that he should have asked the headmaster or allowed the pupils time to ask their parents if they could go to the Lake. It was the end of May and the day was clear and beautiful. The children would certainly love to go for an excursion. After all, the Lake was just another tourist site.

The school children left their bags in their class, got out their lunch packs and snacks for those who had and, together with their teacher, they took the road to the Lake. At the outset, the pupils walked in files of two each and were generally orderly. But by the time they got half way through Mile Twelve, up the hill and towards the mountain where the Lake sits, some of them were tired and were no longer thinking it was such a good idea to go to the Lake after all. However, it was a class excursion and they were with their friends so it made the trip bearable. By the time the children got up to the Lake, most of them were thirsty. The children had barely been around the Lake for thirty minutes, when some of them threw stones into the Lake.

A terrible storm immediately arose and the children ran away. But by the time they got to Santa, the Lake had showed its anger by blowing through Santa, frightening its inhabitants and taking off the roof of all the classes in the government school from which the children came. Since then schools in the neighbouring villages of Santa and Akum take the time to educate their teachers and pupils before venturing on any excursions to Lake Awing. As for the unfortunate teacher, he was frightened to his wits by this *"graffi"* witchcraft and packed his things and moved out of Santa the next day.

As soon as the story of the storm and the destruction of the school in Santa hit the stands and was shown over national television, Pappy wanted to know more.

Lake Awing is situated on a hill overlooking Awing village. A thick forest surrounds Lake Awing with a little outlet running into a stream. It is by the stream that people come and stand in order to see the Lake. The beauty of the Lake is made up of a lot of scenery but the most outstanding thing about the Lake, are the Ducks. If one visited Lake Awing when the Lake was happy, one would see Ducks flying, playing, fluttering, dancing on the surface of the Lake and generally treating you to a show of gymnastics like a modern day ballet troupe.

The Lake moves according to the direction of the wind, making small undulations, gentle whispers as if caressing a lover. But look keenly and you will see that there is a little portion of the Lake that is very dark and still, no matter the direction or the strength of the wind.

The present site of Lake Awing is not its original site. The previous site of the Lake was in *"Achilum"* and by the road to many farms. It was easier for Awing women returning from their farms to stop at the Lake and take a bath rather than get home and send someone to fetch water for them to bathe with. However, the women forgot that a woman menstruating is considered unclean and started bathing even in that unclean state in the Lake. So the Lake got angry about this defilement and decided to move to its present site on top of the hill where no woman would ever have to defile it again. All the inhabitants inside the Lake were not in favour of the move, so one Prince and his family decided to remain on the original site. They are still there today and if you go there, you will see a small body of water nestling at the bottom of the old site of the Lake. That is believed to be the habitat of the Prince and his family who refused to move. At the bottom of the old site of the Lake, footprints and roads are still visible to the naked eye until this day.

Awing is a small village between *Mendankwe, Akum*, and *Santa*. Awing is found in the grass field of the North West Province of Cameroon where most of the scenery is Mountainous. Pleasant to look at, the terrain can be very difficult to exploit. A distance of about fifteen kilometres from *Mankon*, the provincial head quarters of the province, Awing is an ideal village because it is not too near or too far from the cosmopolitan town.

Sacrifices to the Lake are done on a yearly basis. These sacrifices are done during the second week of a particular traditional Sunday during the month of December. The traditional calendar of all villages in the Northwest is eight days. So those who know how to calculate the traditional days of the week can determine the calendar. During the period of sacrificing to the Lake all other activities in the village are suspended. There is no mourning, no weddings, nothing. The entourage that goes to the Lake to present the offerings is done according to neighbourhoods.

In Awing, there are five *"quarters"* or neighbourhoods. Usually, these neighbourhoods are made of many clans put together. At the beginning of the period of offerings to the Lake, the items to offer the lake are collected by the Leader of each neighbourhood, and taken to the palace. At the palace the items are assembled. Then the *"Mbacha"* the notable who goes ahead of the delegation leads the way by ringing a bell which announces that the Fon is going to the Lake, so everyone should make way. The Fon, comes after the Mbacha and is followed by his notables, his Queens, and lastly by all young girls in the village who desire to have children but have not been able to conceive.

At the Lake, some prayers are chanted. Then a goat, which is the main sacrificial item, is cut according to the neighbourhoods and the name of the neighbourhood is called and the part of the goat from them is thrown into the Lake. The Chief priest holds up the piece of goat and says in order of the neighbourhoods.

"Cha Mbetu"

Then throws the meat into the Lake and every one present watches as the Lake comes towards the banks, opens up and the meat is swallowed by the lake.

"Cha Mbedeng"
"Cha Mbejah"
"Cha Mbeten"
"Cha Mbeme"

For each neighbourhood that is called the Lake comes towards its banks to receive the offering. The manner in which the offering is received indicates the Lakes acceptance or refusal. If it comes forward and opens up and receives the offering then the offering has been accepted. If not then there is a problem with that neighbourhood.

After the whole ceremony of sacrifices has been performed, the young ladies desirous of being blessed with fertility are rubbed with camwood. The group is then told to return to the village with strict instructions not to look behind. The reason it is forbidden to look behind is that, the people of Awing believe that every Awing native who dies, goes to settle at the Lake and after the annual sacrifice the dead ancestors escort the group from the Lake back to the village. If anyone disobeys the instructions and looks behind, he or she dies.

The annual sacrifice at the Lake is followed by the *Ndong-Awing* dance, which marks the beginning of festivities in the village. The *Ndong-Awing* lasts for two weeks during which time, all the Fon's children inside and outside the village bring presents to their Fon. The tradition in most Fondoms of the North West is that no one goes to the palace without a present for the Fon. At the same time, since the Fon is every one's father, no one also leaves the palace without a gift from the Fon. So the gifts one person brings can and do usually end up with someone else. However care is taken not to return the same gift to the one who brought the gift.

This two week period during which time all other activities are suspended in the village is used for a cultural bonanza where none-natives can come and be entertained by all the traditional dances and activities taking place at the Fon's palace. Only at the end of this period, can other activities be organised.

The colour of the Lake indicates the state of the economy of the village. When the waters of the Lake are dark, deep and brooding, then the indication is that things will not be good for the children of Awing anywhere. However, when the colour of the Lake, is light, blue and sparkling, then the prognoses are that everything will be fine for the villagers.

Lake Awing is rich in fishes. But the villagers neither eat nor harvest the fish because they believe that they will be eating their ancestors. Neither do they drink the water from the Lake for the same reason. However strangers can swim, fish and carry out other activities at the Lake without any problems.

The belief that all dead Awing people live in the Lake is reinforced by the fact that the villagers say that, at night, the Lake turns into a regular city with a lot of activities taking place. The Lake is supposed to turn back into its normal daylight form before morning. However, sometimes the inhabitants can over sleep and forget to turn back into its lake form. A villager passing by the Lake at daybreak and notices that the houses are still visible simply has to say "the Fon has forgotten himself" and the houses will turn back into the Lake.

It is for this same reason that Awing people do not pass by any road close to the Lake at night. By the same token, the villagers will not pass by the Lake with a corpse, preferring to take a longer road with the corpse even if it would have been shorter to take the road by the Lake. All these villagers do in order to avoid angering the inhabitants of the Lake.

"Mummy" Pappy looked up at me; "You have not finished the story"

"But I just have" I answered him.

"No mum" he replied "You mentioned that there was a dark and still portion of the lake. I think there has to be a reason for that. Isn't there?"

"Well. Yes Pappy but I am surprised you remembered"

"Of course I do Mummy, will you tell me?"

"Okay" I answered and narrated what I had heard.

An argument ensured amongst the inhabitants inside the Lake, because of the defilement by the women. They came from the same clan and most of the inhabitants inside the lake thought they women had defiled the lake deliberately while the other prince and his family thought the women had done it innocently. The angry inhabitants of the Lake inflicted the whole clan with some disease and it killed all the members of the clan. So the inhabitants believe that the dark and still portion of the Lake is the inhabited by the clan, which were all wiped out. As for the prince who remained at the old site of the Lake, he thought that the punishment that the clan received for the crime of the women was too much. So he and his family remained at the old spot while everyone else inside the Lake moved to the new site.

Lake Bosomtwi

"A stream flowed in Eden and watered the garden; beyond Eden it divided into four rivers. The first river is the Pishon; it flows round the country of Havilah. (Pure gold is found there and also rare perfume and precious stones)…. Then the LORD GOD placed the man in the garden to cultivate it and guard it. He said to him, "you may eat the fruit of any tree in the garden, except the tree that gives knowledge of what is good and what is bad. You must not eat the fruit of that tree; if you do, you will die the same day"

Genesis 2:10-12, 15-17

I was sitting next to this Ghanaian young man on the Ethiopian Airlines flight from Douala to Ghana. Ethiopian files ungodly hours, so to be at the airport at three-fifty in the morning meant I had to wake up at three. I had not had enough sleep and was looking forward to catching up on some of that sleep during the flight. That was before I chose my seat on the flight that cold, dark and dreary morning. My companion wanted to chat. He was a businessman travelling from Asia back to his country. And short of changing seats, I could not completely ignore him. Or, he rather decided not to be ignored. Bleary eyed, I listened to him boasting of his beautiful country.

I half-listened to him until the screen started showing our flight route and he pointed out Lake Volta and started talking to me about the Volta region in Ghana. Were there any myths associated with Lake Volta?

I held my breath and waited for the answer but when the answer came, it was a disappointing no! Lake Volta was a man-made lake. Were there any other interesting lakes in Ghana?

83

"Oh yes," the young man answered.

"Can you tell me about it?" I asked

"The one with the most popular myth is Lake Bosomtwi." So saying, he pointed it out to me on the screen. However, there was not much time to hear the story, as the plane was now preparing to land at the Ghanaian International Airport. But my interest had been aroused.

The dream was very vivid. Koffi watched as a creature with wings spread out like those of an eagle, carried him. The creature was half-man and half-animal. It had four legs and two hands. Koffi was sitting on the back of the creature, which was taking him to a destination known only to it. The animal soared through the sky and Koffi could feel the fresh clouds as he was carried above them. The creature passed through some dark clouds and Koffi felt the mist of rain gently brush his face as soft as the feathers of a butterfly.

Then the creature descended to a certain height and Koffi looked down and saw the Earth below him. As he watched, a huge boulder left the sky and shot down towards the Earth. The boulder passed a few feet from where Koffi and the animal were resting and Koffi felt the heat from the boulder as it went shuttling down. Koffi watched as the boulder continued its downward descent until it fell to the Earth and created a big hole in it. Koffi opened his mouth to ask the animal a question, turned on his side and suddenly realised he had been dreaming. He got out of bed. He could not go back to sleep. The dream had been so real. He opened his door to see if it was time for him to go hunting but the night was still too dark and chilly.

Koffi sat on his bed and pondered the dream. As he did so, he touched his arm and felt an unusual pain and liquid on it. Frightened, he stretched his other arm under the bed to search for the paraffin lamp and matches. His hand located the objects and he lit the lamp to see a burn on his arm where before there had not been one. He had not been dreaming, or had he?

Koffi lived on the edge of the forest in the Ashanti region of Ghana. He was a very simple man and had been a hunter all his life. Koffi had no clock and would not have known how to read it had he been given one. He used his senses to tell the time. He could look outside his house, listen to the sounds of the night, feel the wind on his skin and breathe the air to be able to tell if it was   time for him to venture out into the darkness. He had done so all his life and could determine within a few   minutes   of   his waking up if it was time to go out or not.

But that day was different. Koffi had to go hunting because his stock of smoked meat was finished and he needed to replenish it. But he was worried. The burn on his hand, and the dream, worried him. He had to treat the burn with honey before he gauged the time. He would have sworn before that he knew all the animals in the forest and knew most of their names. However, he had never seen anything like the creature he had seen in his dream.

Koffi found the honey under the bed in a metal container blackened by soot and dirt. He scooped some of the honey onto his fingers and smeared it on the burn. The cold feel of the honey melting on Koffi's skin made the hum feel slightly better. Koffi looked at the wound and remembered the dream, which he still could not figure out. Koffi wondered whether he should tie the wound or not? How was he going to put on his animal fur? Should he go out hunting that day or postpone it? If he postponed it, what would he do all day? Was he going to behave like a woman and stay at home all day because of a small burn?

In the end, Koffi put on his trousers that were made of animal skin. Then put on his shoes, which were made of treated elephant hide. He removed his bow and arrow, collected his traditional gun, brought down his hunting bag and hung it across his shoulders and was ready to go. He stepped out of the warmth of his house into the approaching dawn. The cold air hit him on his face, like a physical force. He had forgotten to check the time. He stopped, allowing his eyes to get familiar with the darkness, then sucked in his breath and listened to the sounds of the night. He could hear the cries of crickets, smell the air, which carried a lemon scent. He knew he was about thirty minutes early for his hunting. He stood still and wondered if he should go on or go back into the house and try to sleep. Koffi's dog, which had been sleeping outside, whimpered and got up. That seemed to make up Koffi's mind. He decided to go ahead instead of back into the warmth of the house. He whistled for the dog to follow him, and together, just as on other days, they set off.

He walked on knowing that before he got to his destination the mildew on the grass would have rubbed off on his legs and made them wet. He had trodded the road so many times that his feet knew the stones and the pebbles, and his eyes could see the stumps before he got near them. Koffi walked on, and long before he reached it, he could smell a scent in the air that was different from anything he had ever smelled in his life. Koffi stopped. That smell! Where was it coming from and what did it remind him of? The smell was acrid. It was a mixture of burning skin and heat. The smell reminded Koffi of something. What? He searched his mind, and remembered the dream. Curious, Koffi forgot about hunting and let his nostrils lead him to where the smell was coming from.

Koffi walked on. And as the smell got stronger, so too did the air get warmer. Koffi was confused. What was he leading himself into? Night gave way to daybreak just as Koffi got to the area and saw lying before him in all ethereal beauty, a large pool of water.

Koffi stood at the edge of the water and tried to see the end of the water but as far as his eyes could stretch, there was no end to the water. He scooped some of the water into his palms and it was so cool to touch. The water was real, after all. It was not a dream. Koffi splashed some of the water onto the burn on his arm and watched as the place healed before his eyes, leaving only a tiny scar to remind him of the dream. He was either dreaming or dead and his spirit was floating in space. Koffi looked at his feet. He was standing on earth. He could breathe and feel. All his senses were alert. So what was happening to him? Koffi had landed on a find, and had to go and inform "Nana" the Chief. It was fully bright now. Koffi saw that the lake was full of fish; he caught some of the fish and gave it to his dog, who ate it and did not die. Koffi pushed any thoughts of hunting out of his mind and returned to the village, heading straight for the palace.

Koffi waited outside and asked for audience with the chief as soon as the Chief woke up and could receive people. The Chief came out and sat on his seat in his audience room and immediately asked for Koffi to be brought in. Koffi entered the room trembling. It was Koffi's first time to be that close to the Chief. He opened his mouth to say what he had come to tell the Chief, but no words seemed to come out. He looked to the Chief's advisers for help, but none was forthcoming from that area. He took a deep breath, and then explained as best he could, what he had come to say.

To the astonishment of the few people present at the palace at that time of the morning, the Chief asked for his anointing oil and said, "I saw the *old wise one* in my dream last night. You are the one he asked me to anoint. You are to be the Sub-Chief of the lake and all the area around it. The people there will be your subjects and the lake will belong to you and your children forever."

In most African countries, traditional rulers are believed to have special powers. They have natural powers by being born of nobility, but when one is made Chief, then the powers of his ancestors are conferred on him and it us believed that they can communicate with those ancestors, which is how they acquire the wisdom to rule the country well. But, as yet, no one had heard of a Chief who could communicate with the *"old wise one."*

Koffi and the other people could hardly believe what they were hearing. Had their Chief gone senile? But given the powers that they were imbued with, no Chief had ever gone senile before. As for Koffi, he felt some relief because the dream and everything he had gone through, were real.

The Chief sent messengers out to call the elders of the tribe to come and participate in the installation rites of the new Chief of the Ashanti region.

The people were asked to bring cows, goats, chickens, four, maize and lots of food to the palace. Celebrations were going to take place for a week, and the week was declared a period of festivities. All the traditional dances would come out on a daily basis in their order of importance. The women were all preparing food to entertain local and foreign dignitaries, while the young girls smoothed cocoa butter fat on their hair and skin and hoped to catch the eye of some young man.

During all that time, Koffi stayed at the palace. He had been given a special chamber at the palace and only came out during the day to take his place besides the Chief. The Chief had provided him with expensive traditional gear. Koffi was scared. He was a simple hunter whose life had changed within the twinkle of an eye. Was he going to be up to the task of doing what he was being asked to do? Why had the gods, if he understood well, chosen him?

During the day, there were traditional dances, festivities and parades of young virgins attired in heads and nothing else, their breast and young bodies oiled until they were glistening. Koffi had to choose anyone of the virgins to be his wife. There were so many young nubile virgins that making a choice was not so easy for Koffi. There were notables who pushed their daughters forward in the hope of becoming the new Sub-Chief's father-in-law in order to enjoy the facilities that went with such positions. In the end, Koffi chose a light-skinned girl who looked ripe and succulent. At the end of the week-long celebrations, Koffi and his new bride were escorted to their new home a few miles from the lake. Able-bodied young men who had been specially chosen to be his escorts, carried Koffi in a palanquin. That tradition has, therefore, remained with each generation of the Ashanti Chiefs to this day.

Apparently, while the festivities had been going on, the Chief had sent some young men to go ahead and build a new house for the new Sub-Chief. That is how Koffi became the first Sub-Chief of the lake, which was named Botsomtwi, meaning, *'a million gods.'*

Most traditional African Chiefs do not share sleeping quarters with their wives because tradition supposes they will be polygamous. There is also the question of women not being allowed near certain traditional ornaments during their menstrual cycles because menses would defile the ornament. The young men had, therefore, within that one-week, built two houses for Koffi.

After Koffi settled, it was left to him to arrange the building of his palace the way he wanted, depending on the number of wives and children he intended to have. Koffi found gold along the banks of the lake and his goldsmiths made what has come to be known as the famous golden stool of the Ashanti *Asantene.* Chief Koffi married many wives, was blessed with many children and he expanded his palace and made the lake and its inhabitants famous beyond their boundaries. However, when Nana, the supreme Chief of the Ashanti Kingdom who anointed Koffi, died, his successor was not happy with Koffi's prosperity. A war ensued which only ended with the fusion of the two kingdoms. That is why today there is only one Ashanti King.

Lake Bosomtwi is found in the Ashanti region of Ghana, five hours' drive from Accra, the capital of Ghana.

It is one of the biggest lakes in Africa, and covers a surface area of over four miles. In the olden days, it used to be said truthfully too that one could not see the end of the lake from any side of it. It takes two days to walk round the lake. The lake has since become a touristic attraction, and so the government has built campsites and provided hotel facilities round the lake.

The lake produces fish of all kinds. The fish all look black in colour and are so delicious they can be eaten down to the bones. Fishing is allowed in the lake every day except on Tuesdays. It is believed that if any one fishes in the lake on Tuesdays, they will sec something which they are not meant to see, and that can result in their death. On Tuesdays, there should be no swimming or other activities around the lake. However, for touristic purposes, the lake is open on Tuesdays, but not for fishing.

From the origins of the lake, it is believed that the lake contains some powers, so the people around it live in awe of the lake. The descendants of the hunter Koffi, who found the lake, perform rites and sacrifices to the lake. The Chief finds out from the lake through special communications if the lake needs something. Then the Chief carries whatever it is that the lake needs together with cows, sheep and 'akpteshi' a potent local brew. The Chief takes the things to the lake, offers a prayer on behalf of his people, and then, one after the other, he throws the things into the lake and watches how the lake receives them and from that he knows if the sacrifices are accepted or not.

Lake Bosomtwi, which in normal circumstances behaves like the sea, with strong waves moving from the lake to the shore and back, is still when a sacrifice is being offered. The waves stand still as if listening to the demands of the people. After the sacrifice, the lake moves back and one can note from the motion of the waves, if the lake is happy or not. It is said that the Chief can probably communicate with the lake, but onlookers can only watch the waves. If the waves are strong, then a roaring sound like that of a lion can be heard, signifying that the lake is not satisfied. But if the lake is happy, then the waves are gentle and a quiet sound like that of a purring cat can be heard. In that case, everyone leaves from there happy.

During the many centuries the lake has existed, no one remembers a time when the lake was not happy with its sacrifices because it is consulted before the sacrifices are offered. However, when the lake is angry, it defends itself and metes out the punishment the perpetrator merits without wasting time.

The story goes that the son of a fisherman who had gone to school but decided to return home, settle and expand his father's business, decided to go fishing on a Tuesday because they had an unusually large amount of order from a customer the previous day. Without telling his wife or father, he decided to set out fishing alone. He got to the lake, untied his boat and went about his trade. He had barely gone a quarter of the way when he saw lines of golden geese swimming across the lake. The geese stopped and one addressed him, "You have seen what you came to see, haven't you?"

The young man was trembling. He did not know where the line of golden geese had come from, let alone the fact that they could speak. He could not answer, so the goose continued, "Go back, you will not find any fish today. Whether you tell anyone what you have seen here or not, does not matter because you will still die."

The young man returned home without any fish, told his story, and died. That confirmed to the inhabitants, beyond any more doubts, the good sense of staying away from the lake on Tuesdays.

Lake Mfoû

The LORD said to Abram, "Leave your country, your relatives, and your father's home, and go to a land that I am going to show you. I will give you many descendants, and they will become a great nation. I will bless you and make your name famous, so that you will be a blessing."

Genesis, 12:1-2

It would have been the last route we should have taken during that particular time of the year, because there had been persistent reports of highway robbers attacking and killing people on that route. However, we got to Bafoussam late and not wanting to go through Bamenda and sleep on the way, we decided to risk going through the Foumban route, which in hindsight was a foolhardy thing to do.

As if risking our lives was not enough, the car had a flat tire a few metres from *"Ferme de Kunden"* or more precisely, Kunden Farmhouse. The driver removed the spare tire and found that it was also flat. How this could have happened, I did not want to think about otherwise I would lose my temper. While the driver was looking for someone to help him show a tire repair place, I walked over to the farmhouse, admired its simple design and architecture and then walked back and found a spot next to a man sitting in front of a bar and ordered a coke.

The West Province is all virtually farm country and has been called the breadbasket of Cameroon and the Central African sub region. I looked at the farmhouse again and must have wondered aloud what a farmhouse was doing by the side of the road when my neighbour said, "Buy me a beer and I will tell you the story."

93

I took a closer look at the man. He was about seventy years old. He was wearing a hand woven jumper, the cheap kind one can see in about any market on the West Coast of Africa; and on his head was a black cap with a red feather, which only notables in that part of the region wore. I hesitated a little bit, but noticed that hanging on his neck too were the huge blue and white beads which notables of a certain status wore. Had I been more observant at the beginning, I probably would have chosen a different seat because women are not normally allowed to sit next to notables of that caliber. I was not sure what to do at that point. I would buy him the drink, but was I supposed to move away? If I did, how would I hear the story if indeed there was one?

I called the bartender and asked him to give my neighbour a beer of his choice. The bartender brought him a large cold Guinness without bothering to ask his choice. The man who introduced himself to me as Njimolu, took a sip of the beer then said, "You see, that farmhouse was built at its present site because it could not be built at the place where it was supposed to be built."

"Where was it supposed to be built?" I asked

"It was originally planned to be built close to Lake Mfoû.

"Then what happened?"

"The gods of the lake refused to have it built there."

"How come?"

'It is a long story" he replied.

"I have all the time in the world; besides, you promised to tell me the story for a beer which you are already drinking."

"Okay" he answered with a crooked smile, daring me to see if I would have either the time or the stomach for the story he was about to tell me:

Lake Mfoû is one of two lakes that originated from a volcanic eruption of Mount Mpapit sometime in the thirteenth century. The two lakes, male and female, had neither significance nor special importance except as a water source. However, during the fifteenth century, something happened that made the female lake, Mfoû, have magical powers. Lake Mfoû is situated some eight kilometres from Foumbot town under the foot of Mount Mbapit in a little village called Ngbetnsouen. From the edge, one descends about two hundred and thirty metres before seeing the surface of the lake, which is nestled in boulder-like surroundings. It is believed that it could take more than seven hours to walk round the lake.

Before the fifteenth century, what is known as the *Noun* Division today was inhabited by the Bên people and the place was called Fompabên, which simply meant, home of the Bên. Believed to be water people because their gods resided in water, the Bên were a peaceful but powerful tribe until the fourteenth century when the great Bamoun conqueror, Nchare Yen, left his homeland of the Tikar in the North and fought his way southwards. The Tikars were hunters and fishermen who were tall and fearless warriors. After the death of the father of Prince Nchare Yen, the throne was disputed between him and his brother, and the young and proud prince Nchare left Tikar with his faction of supporters and defeated many villages and tribes on the way South.

When they got to Fompabên and saw the lush fresh green grass, they decided to settle there. However, there was strong resistance from the Bêns who themselves were great warriors. Chief Mfopit and his men put up a strong fight, which lasted many months. In the end, the Bêns were no match for the strong Tikars. The Tikars, wearing long animal skins round their waist and holding shields and long two pointed spears, with painted faces and many necklaces and good luck talismans, frightened the Bêns who in their time had been very good warriors.

The Fon of the Bên, Chief Mfopit, was captured and so when surrender was imminent, seven notables with supernatural powers took refuge in the female lake rather than be captured and taken as slaves. After the notables entered the lake, a different kind of battle between them and the Bamoun began. Chief Nchare Yen and his people could not enjoy their victory. Every night, a different kind of battle was fought between the people in the lake and the Bamoun. At night there was neither sleep nor rest for Chief Nchare. He summoned his traditional soothsayers who all told him that the only way to settle peacefully was to go and talk with the "spirits" in the lake. Chief Nchare, together with some of his notables, duly took offerings to the lake and the lake told them that the only way to have peace was not to treat the captives as slaves and to hive in mutual respect. Chief Nchare Yen was forced to accept the conditions of the lake. Since then, it is believed that the lake has mystical powers. When Chief Mfopit died in captivity, it is believed that the notables took his soul and kept it in the lake; and after him, any notable of the Bên descent who dies is taken to hive in the lake.

The Ben people believe that their ancestors inhabit the lake so nothing can be thrown inside the lake. But should anyone try, the object would not fall into the lake. It will return and fall outside the lake. It is also believed that ram falls around the lake but never into it. Within a certain radius of the lake, people are not allowed to build or farm. People who try to build within this radius, find it difficult to do so and even if they succeed in building, they cannot live in the house.

"Why?" I interrupted to ask.

"People who previously succeeded in doing so found that when they went to sleep at night with their doors locked and bolted from the inside, would find all the doors wide-open in the morning. Sometimes, people slept in their houses and when they woke up in the morning, they found themselves outside their houses."

"I would understand that frightening people away, but what about the Kunden farmhouse?" I further inquired.

"Some Europeans came to establish their business in this area and decided to build a farmhouse. The Europeans brought their architects and labour from Europe; and when they came, they decided to build the house near the lake. The villagers told them they could not because the gods would not allow them to do so, but they simply laughed and went ahead to draw their plans and came to start the building. No villager would accept to work for the building company so they brought in people from other Provinces to work on the building. They started digging to lay the foundation, saw a large python and some of the workers ran away. They got more workers, and succeeded in digging the trenches for the foundation. They worked all day, went home to rest in the night, but when they came in the morning, they found that the foundation had collapsed. This went on for three months after which the white men accepted that African witchcraft was stronger than theirs and left the dwelling place of the gods to come and build the house where it currently stands. Today, one can still find part of the abandoned foundation where the white men left it."

Njimolu finished his beer as the twilight was giving way to the darkness of the night. Since I wanted to hear more of the story, I bought him another beer and asked, "What evidence is there that the gods of the lake are actually there or responsible for ah you said?"

He chuckled a little, showing tobacco-stained teeth, and then looked at me for a little while. I was wondering if he was going to respond, when he answered, "Plenty."

The traditional market days in most Cameroonian villages comes up every eight days, a practice which still prevails today in most villages. This market system allowed the mostly farming villagers the opportunity to work their farms during the other days, take their produce to the market, sell them and buy whatever additional commodities they needed. Legend has it that on one market day many years ago, a woman left the mountain area and went to a nearby market around Baigom, which is about four kilometres from Foumbot. At the end of the day, tired, thirsty and not having eaten anything all day, she strapped her baby on her back, carried her com on her head and when she arrived Baigom village, she begged for water to drink but was denied the water. Angry, frustrated and tired, she walked up to the lake and putting her basket of corn down, she sat to rest and told the gods of the lake her story with the people of Baigom. The following day, when the people of Baigom woke up, their source of water, which was a river, had changed course and was diverted to another village known as Masset. Until this day, the dried up riverbed in Baigom is there for anyone to see.

"What did the people of Baigom do?"

"What could they do? They went to the lake with sacrifices to apologize and make amends, but they knew that the anger of the gods, especially for a wrong done towards a woman and child, is difficult to appease."

"Then why did they bother?"

"They had to because the other repercussions from the lake could have been more devastating."

"I would not want to make the lake angry with me."

"You had better not" Njimolu said with another chuckle, which I was beginning to get used to and to like. "People who have tried have been heavily punished."

People around here know that they should not farm near the lake because although the land around there looks lush and green, nothing will grow there. On the one hand, it would disturb the spirits and on the other hand, it would mean too frequent access to the lake and one could see something the lake does not want them to see.

There existed a man who thought he had the power and spiritual strength to work near the lake. He went and started farming there. He tilled from morning until dusk and returned home. The following morning, he returned to the place and there was no sign that the earth had even been disturbed there. Puzzled, he continued to till. At sunset, before returning home, he put a red marker on the spot where he had ended work. The following morning, he found that the red marker was still there but the earth had been covered back as if nothing had ever been touched. Determined, he took his shovel and tried to dig again and a large two-headed snake came out from the soil and swallowed him. If one visits the spot even now, the red marker can still be seen.

"So even hunting is not allowed near the lake?" I asked.

"Hunting is allowed only for food but never for anything else. However, if the purpose of the hunting is anything other than hunger, then the hunter would not find any animal and might end up being the hunted instead."

"Wow!" I exclaimed. Njimolu was on his third beer and I was beginning to worry where we would spend the night as it was now out of question for us to travel to Nso that night. At the same time, I wanted to let Njimolu finish his narrative but before I could say anything, the old man uttered softly, so softly that I almost missed it with the noise and bustle of the people in the bar and the music blaring away from a nearby local disco,

"You weren't meant to get there today."

"What did you say?" I asked a little frightened.

"Never mind, call your driver and ask him to go and book you for the night in the hotel that is just round the corner" he virtually ordered.

Did I do as he asked because I wanted to hear the rest of the lake story or was it because I already did not feel like continuing that night? I was asking myself all these questions and started yawning just when my driver returned.

The old man then said, "You have an early day tomorrow and am an old man. It is time you went to bed and time for me to return home. Thank you for the drinks."

"Thank you instead, it was nice talking to you" I reassured him.

"Good night" he said.

"Good night" I replied, and followed my driver to the hotel.

The next morning, I got up at six and as I turned on the radio, there was a report of highway robbery on the Foumban route, an incident in which three people had been shot dead.

Lake Aheme

"One of the twelve disciples, Thomas (called the twin), was not with them when Jesus came. So the other disciples told him, "We have seen the Lord."

Thomas said to them, "Unless I see the scars of the nails in his hands and put my finger on those scars and my hand in his side, I will not believe."

John 20:24-25

The night before he travelled, Jansen Van der Meer was having second thoughts. He lay in bed sleepless. He could hear his girlfriend of the past five years asking him, "What would happen to us if you go to Africa?"

"I don't know Jean" Jansen answered truthfully.

"Do you expect me to wait for you for two years while you trapeze in some African jungle and bring back God knows what?"

"I hope you will Jean."

"Well, what if I cannot?"

The arguments were happening so often during the past weeks that Jansen, already exasperated, answered,

"If you can't Jean, then it wasn't meant to be."

"You mean you are willing to throw away everything we have built together on this hay brain idea of yours?"

"It's just something I feel I want to do at this point in my life. I'd hoped you would understand. I'd hoped you would also wait. But if you cannot, then I do not know what to say, but I will understand."

Jean had stormed out in a rage and Jansen was now wondering if he was indeed doing the right thing and if he could have been gentler with her. If the truth must be known,

Jansen was excited but scared at the same time. His parents had worked overseas before and were also scared for him, but they had given him their full support. Jansen wished he could have had the support of his girlfriend too. Was the service lie was about to plunge into worth ail the sacrifice lie was going to make?

The twenty-year-old Dutch, Jansen van der Meer, had been in Benin for two months and was walking along the road with his new *Beninois* friend, Koffo. They got to the edge of the forest and Koffo crossed the road to the other side, and quickened his steps while making the sign of the cross on his forehead. Jansen crossed the road too and had to run to catch up with Koffo, and they continued on their way. Jansen noticed that each time lie invited Koffo to walk with him, lie would do the same thing when they came to the edge of the forest. Puzzled, he asked Koffo why lie did that.

"Forest too frightful" Koffo answered.

"What do you mean too frightful?" Jansen asked.

'Witches, too many bad things happen to people near the forest. I no like to go near."

"African nonsense" Jansen said.

Koffo did not answer but continued to walk away from the forest.

Jansen was a young, blonde, blue-eyed Dutch volunteer in the Dahomey town of Allada during the early sixties. Out of college for barely a year, he had joined the Dutch Volunteer Service Overseas as some sort of adventure. The advertisement asking for applicants had given the impression that volunteers were going to teach citizens of the former French colony some basic sanitary ideas, and do some cultural exchange. Jansen was one amongst many youths who applied because they did not have an idea what they wanted to do with their lives at that particular time. Therefore, a paid two-year vacation to Africa was not a bad deal.

It was on a hot day in July of 1960, just after Benin gained its independence from France that the young Jansen and fourteen other Dutch nationals arrived in Cotonou, the economic capital of Benin. The first thing that surprised them was that the African country which they had thought was mostly wild forest had a proper airport and people were dressed in "normal" clothes, instead of animal skins or worse yet, running around naked. They were in for other surprises. But their tenure was already promising to be an exciting one. After a one-month briefing in the capital city, the new volunteers were sent off to their different posts to work alone or meet other volunteers on the field.

Jansen was sent to Guézin, a village not far from Allada town. He was, therefore, not far from the capital city, Porto-Novo, where the Dutch Ambassador lived. Jansen was fortunate that there was another Dutch volunteer in the village and so they quickly became friends. The other volunteer - who had already spent one year in the country - could show Jansen around and made his stay comfortable by finding a house for Jansen that was not far from his.

James Nielen liked the local colour and had made friends with the villagers. It, therefore, became easy for Jansen to have Koffo as a friend, who accompanied him and sometimes translated for him because Jansen had to work occasionally with natives who knew none of the foreign languages Jansen could speak. During those times, the need for a translator was quite of essence.

After one of his morning walks, Jansen met James and told him the odd behaviour of Koffo each time they were walking.

"I have been told that there is a beautiful lake in the forest. But I have never been there, because the forest is considered sacred" James answered.

"You mean you have been here for a year and not gone to see the lake?" Jansen asked.

"The procedure to get into the forest just seemed too difficult and complicated for me." James answered.

"I would like to go there" Jansen declared.

"I would advise you to talk with Koffo to make the necessary arrangements" James admonished.

"Will you come with me or do you believe all this African nonsense about witchcraft and bad spirits in the forest?" Jansen asked.

"Jansen, I am not sure what I believe but am curious enough to want to go into the forest. So let's see how we make the arrangements and we can go on a Saturday" James replied.

"Okay. I will discuss this with Koffo and get back to you" Jansen replied.

Koffo insisted that he could not go with them to the forest but he could take them to the house of the Chief Priest to obtain permission to visit the forest. They went to the Chief Priest's house at about four in the afternoon on a Sunday. The house was made of mud, built with sticks and thatched with thin grass. The house was round and did not seem to have any partitions. The one-room house served as kitchen, bedroom, and meeting room -everything in one. The entrance to the house was low and narrow but Koffo made a loud sound and a scruffy voice answered from within and Koffo answered back in the dialect. Then he told James and Jansen to follow him inside.

The room was smoky and had no windows. The old man cleared his throat and welcomed his guests through Koffo, who interpreted to the guests. He offered them seats made with bamboo. Then he brought out kola nuts from under his bed and 'sodabi', a local whisky made from palm wine and offered these to the guests. Jansen looked at the soot-covered containers and was going to refuse but James nudged him on the side and told him it would be rude to refuse. So they gracefully accepted the drinks. After watching them sip the drinks, the Chief Priest then asked them why they had come to see him.

"We would like to visit the forest and see the lake" they answered, Koffo interpreting for them.

"You can go into the forest" the Chef Priest answered, "anytime before sunset, between Thursdays and Saturdays. You can see whatever you want to see. But you are not allowed to take pictures of the lake. Furthermore, you have to bring me two white cocks and a goat, two bottles of gin and some money for me to offer to the gods before you can go in."

Jansen and James left the hut with hearts beating and wondering what they had gotten themselves into. They had heard stories of Lake Aheme and wanted to see it but what was the cost going to be? They were just volunteers and although they earned more than the highest paid civil servant in Benin, they still did not earn enough to allow them to spend their money on "tourism." Lake Aheme was not a mere fancy though.

They, therefore, sent the items to the Chief Priest and decided to set off for the forest on a cold Saturday morning. Within hours after leaving the home of the Chief Priest, word had gone round about their intentions. When they passed, people pointed at them and whispered, but it did not bother them. They were used to being stared at, called *"le blanc or Yovo"*, and more so, they always stood out in the sea of black faces.

Jansen said, "I am going to slow these niggers. They think they are smart. Tell me how is that old man going to know if we took pictures of the lake or not?"

On the day of the visit, Jansen and James both took their Nikon cameras. Jansen put his camera in his bag and tore a round hole from which he could take pictures without anyone seeing him do so. James put his own camera in the pocket of his jeans and also cut a hole in it. They were happy and ready to go and discover the African fairy tale!

Lake Aheme is located in the Southern part of Benin and occupies a surface of about 78 square kilometres. The Pedah and the Ayizo tribes migrated to the area to take refuge from the ferocious king Agadja of the Abomey tribe who conquered them and occupied their territory. With both Pedah and the Ayizo tribes depending on the lake for fishing subsistence, quarrels started and would have ensued into war but for the timely arrival of a hunter called Eklousse. He left his village, Niaouli and arriving at Guezin, killed two panthers which terrified both tribes. He was made king and given the name *Deh Zounon*. He brought peace and unity to the two tribes.

The *Deh Zounon* took control of the voodoos and spiritual representations of the lake gods. After consultations with the gods, it was forbidden to jump into the lake, because the spirits inhabiting the lake would be angry and punish the violator. During the special periods for the sacrifices for protecting the lake, fishing was not allowed and sanctions for violators ranged from punishment to death. The power of witchcraft, magic and spiritual punishment rested in the hands of the chief priests and certain old men in the village. When any violator was killed, his body would be dragged through the village as a deterrent to other violators. Various people had told James and Jansen all these stories but they still wanted to go to the lake and see.

Jansen and James entered the forest and started walking in the general directions they had been given to get to the lake. It was daylight but they were holding flashlights because they had been informed accurately that some parts of the forest would be so dark that they would not be able to see their way clearly.

An animal growled close by and James held Jansen's hand.

"This may not have been a very good idea after all. What happens if we get lost in here?" James asked.

"I hope they will send people to come and look for us." Jansen replied.

"God, Jan, I hope these people do not end up using us for their voodoo practices."

"Now you have frightened me," said Jansen, shivering. Jansen could not forget his first contact with the "voodoo" and still shivered when he remembered it. He looked at his hands and noticed he had goose bumps, and his hands were actually shaking.

Two months after he had started doing his volunteer service, he had scheduled a meeting with a community at four in the afternoon. He arrived at the site and saw that a crowd had actually gathered. Jansen thought the crowd was waiting for him to come and talk to them about hygiene, mosquitoes and healthy living. That would have been a first because amongst other things, Jansen had learned that standard African time was different from European time. But when they got close, they could see that the faces of the spectators were painted with black lines and there was a young naked girl lying in the middle of the circle, next to burning wood. The people were chanting some incantations. Afraid that the people with the spears were going to kill the girl, Jansen had run into the middle before Koffo had time to stop him. In the process, he was attacked by the participants and could have been killed but for Koffo's intervention. After that, Jansen stayed far away when he heard any chanting. But the affair shocked him so badly he had almost taken the next plane home.

"James" Jansen said, "You just gave me a good reason to return, but I am not going to do so without reaching the lake."

"Okay, buddy, let's continue" James said.

James and Jansen heard the sound before they saw the animal. The grass was opening up on their left and the hoofs of the animal shook the underbrush. James held Jansen's hand and whispered "Stand still" and they stood and waited as the huge elephant carne into view but moved away from them. Jansen held his breath and only released it after the elephant stood a distance from them. When they released their hands, their palms were wet with sweat and fear.

"Did we just miss an opportunity to take a picture?" Jansen asked.

"The elephant is still within view, let's take the picture" James said.

They continued on their way, taking pictures of monkeys, wild flowers and anything that caught their fancy. They reached the lake at the end of the trek and the beauty of the green lush water in the middle of a thick forest rendered them speechless and awestruck. The huge body of water lay as far as the eye could see, surrounded by grass and trees of magnificent height. There was no debris in the lake, and white ducks flapped their wings, swimming from one end to the other, performing a mating dance to the tranquil music of the lake.

Jansen and James looked at each other and both pressed their cameras and took pictures upon pictures. They thought it was a shame for these Africans to want to keep such splendour all to themselves because of some stupid beliefs.

Jansen said, "I want to sit here for a while and just enjoy this."

James added, "Same here, and while we are at it, we may eat our lunch. But remember not to throw anything into the lake or leave something lying around."

"As if I could forget" Jansen said, "we should make sure we do not stay too long too, so we can get out before the spirits go prowling about."

"If the lake was not so beautiful, I would say we should leave even now" James said.

The way back was uneventful, James and Jansen were happy they had outsmarted their hosts. As soon as they reached their respective homes, they ran to their dark rooms to develop their films. Jansen developed the film and hung it up and looked...then looked again. On the roll of film, there were pictures of everything he had snapped in the forest but there was nothing that even remotely resembled a lake. He could not believe it. He called James and said, "James, I hope your pictures of the lake came out. My camera had a malfunction."

To his dismay, James answered, "If your camera had a malfunction, then so did mine. The films of the lake are all blank." The two friends practically heard their heart's beating as they replaced the phones.

Three months later, both of them had to go to Porto-Novo, the capital, to see the Dutch Ambassador. When they recounted their experience of the lake, the Ambassador answered, "Are you trying to tell me that I can take my new Nikon camera, with new films and batteries and go to Lake Aheme, take pictures and nothing will come out?"

"Your Excellency, why don't you try it out yourself?" asked Jansen.

"I would not even dare a thing like that in this country. You boys are lucky you came out alive to tell the story."

What do you think? Was it mystique or just a coincidental malfunction of two cameras?